WHERE WE ARE, WHAT WE SEE

THE BEST YOUNG ARTISTS AND WRITERS IN AMERICA

A **PUSH** ANTHOLOGY

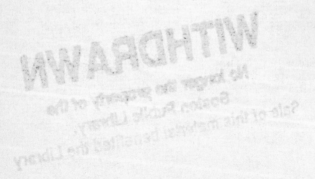

WHERE WE ARE, WHAT WE SEE

THE BEST YOUNG ARTISTS AND WRITERS IN AMERICA

A **PUSH** ANTHOLOGY

EDITED BY DAVID LEVITHAN

SCHOLASTIC INC.

NEW YORK TORONTO LONDON AUCKLAND SYDNEY

MEXICO CITY NEW DELHI HONG KONG BUENOS AIRES

ISBN 0-439-73646-3

All rights reserved. Published by PUSH, an imprint of Scholastic Inc., 557 Broadway, New York, NY 10012.

12 11 10 9 8 7 6 5 4 3 2 1   5 6 7 8 9 10/0

Printed in the U.S.A.   40
First Scholastic/PUSH printing, May 2005

Editor's Note

It should go without saying, but it doesn't really get said nearly enough: Art matters. Writing matters. In a world that is constantly derailing from what we expect our world to be, in lives that are constantly confounding in ways both wonderful and terrible, words and images give us so many things. Expression. Observation. Interpretation. A sense that there is something we can control. Something we can create.

The stories, poems, essays, and artwork in this anthology were chosen from the hundreds of winners of the 2002, 2003, and 2004 Scholastic Art & Writing Awards. All of the writers and artists are middle school or high school students. And they all share an ability to work their words and their art into something that matters. These are all artists who are engaged in the world around them, some during the smallest of moments, some in the face of the largeness of history and mortality. They have both insight and the ability to convey this insight to another person — a reader, a viewer, a holder of beliefs and thoughts. By showing us themselves, they show us ourselves . . . and vice versa.

I would like to thank the people who made this anthology possible, in ways that truly matter. Jeff Brown, Christopher Krovatin, Nicholas Eliopulos, Annmarie Nye, and Joshua Glazer were all vital parts of the selection process, each taking a share in reviewing the thousands of pages that needed to be narrowed down into this collection. Alex Tapnio, Chuck

Wentzel, B.J. Adler, and all of the other amazing people at the Scholastic Art & Writing Awards have provided the spirit of this endeavor, which is fueled by their remarkable program. Steve Scott is the wonderful art director responsible for the art side of this book, and our absolutely perfect production editor, Bonnie Cutler, helped push it through in fine form.

Most of all, I would like to thank the artists and writers you will find on the following pages. May this be just the beginning of a long life of creation for each of you, and may you always realize that what you do matters.

— David Levithan

For more information about PUSH, please go to
www.thisispush.com

To find out more about
the Scholastic Art & Writing Awards
check out
www.scholastic.com/artandwriting

Table of Contents

WHERE WE ARE, WHAT WE SEE

THE BEST YOUNG ARTISTS AND WRITERS IN AMERICA

A **PUSH** ANTHOLOGY

Canvas

An old girlfriend would always write on my skin,
in blue or black ink. We both knew she was destined
to be a tattoo artist, though she never would admit it.
Little yin-yangs, tulips, messages like why
are you so nervous, or decisive, or spontaneous.
I let her write a poem down my spine
with a sharp black ballpoint
and never found out what it said. It used to tickle
so much that she would get mad at me
for ruining the shapes. I got used to it though,
when the skin art became our ritual of afterplay,
and we kept a pen on the table beside the bed.
When she drew a stick figure angel
in between two little clouds on my thigh,
I took the pen from her and scribbled
"Don't fake orgasms"
on her rib cage.
Eventually we broke up
because the ink was soaking in and poisoning
the whims, revealing that we didn't really love
each other. Years later I walked into her tattoo
parlor, on a side street in Chicago.
She smiled to see that I had tracked her down,
but put a finger to my lips. She sat me down
without a word and began stabbing my forearm
with her little machine. When she was done

there was an intricate human heart
you could almost see beating,
colorless and real. It hurt more than I'd expected.
"Don't worry about the girls," she said.
"Anyone who can't understand that
doesn't deserve you."

— Dylan Ravenfox

Hundred Percent Virgin

She's lying
by the window
nude
except for
the sweater
and slacks
and
polka-dotted socks
and
scarf

thinking about sex

it must enter
your mind
sometime
and now it has crept
into
hers
not entirely by mistake
but just
because

they called her virgin today

this bothers her
how could
someone
comment on
such a thing

even though it's true

she's been thinking about
the lack of "it"
for long enough
a mind reader
was bound to
come along

virgin hair

never
been dyed
virgin nails
never
been polished
virgin eyes
never
seen anything

of sexual importance except in bio

sunbeams
leap through
the window
it is the warmest she's gotten
since
the hug
from Angela's brother
and that doesn't even count

because his parents told him to

— Elena Grill

Shades of Red

Sometimes I feel out of place here, being the only one not on antidepressants, being the only one with a measurable level of emotional stability.

My mother is telling me again about how she wishes she could kill herself. How if it weren't for me, she'd take a razor to her wrists. How I'm her only reason for remaining on this earth. What really scares me is she doesn't just say this in a fit of tears anymore; she wears a completely straight face.

I don't know what to do, again, so I do what I always do when I don't know what to do. I hug, and hold her hand. When you don't know how to give someone comfort through words, your only option is to make them feel safe physically, enveloped.

The first time she told me she wanted to kill herself I wasn't very worried. The nerve damage in her leg had flared up and she was screaming in pain. She just wanted a gun, she said. This was worse than giving birth. Only giving birth goes away. She'll feel like someone's twisting a knife in her thigh until her medication kicks in, at least once a week, for the rest of her life. At the moment, she just wanted the pain to stop, any way possible. But this is different.

This time, the past few times, it's been about my stepdad, David. It's been whenever he comes up. It's been almost every day.

Last week he told her, basically, that he wasn't interested in anything she had to say. Admittedly, when someone spends twenty-three-and-a-half hours of her day in bed, she doesn't usually have stories to tell that keep a person on the edge of his seat. But when you care about someone, I've always thought that you listen anyway. I spend two hours a day with my mom. He can't stand to listen to her voice while he piddles around with his computer games. Can't she just shut up for just one minute, he asks.

So that leaves me here, in the kitchen, where David's dinner dishes from three nights ago are sitting on the table, food rotting on them. He can't seem to grasp the idea of cleaning up after himself, and it's not my place to reveal this novel idea to him. I pick up the dish and wash it.

He hasn't been taking his medication, she tells me. I say I know.

This marriage is just so she can still raise my little sister, Katy, she says. I say I know.

She has to try to fix all the ways he's fucking her up. She has his manic depression, his sloppiness, his selfishness, she says. I say I know.

I want to say I don't know. I don't know anything. I don't know what to tell her to do, or what to do myself. I scrub dishes with everything in me. Somehow I've equated fixing the messes David leaves around the house with fixing all the other things he breaks, like my mom. But suggesting a mop bucket will fix a marriage is ridiculous.

She doesn't know what to do, she says. He wasn't like this when she married him, she says. I say I know, and this time I do. I remember. Nothing used to be this way.

I hear the front door open. She starts to head back to bed. I tell her I have homework and applications to fill out, I have to practice piano, I have laundry to do.

Okay, she says. She doesn't know what she'd do without me, she says.

Upstairs, I'm filling out a scholarship application. Date of birth, name of high school, social security number. I feel normal for just a second, the rest of the house quiet and me alone doing something I'm sure millions of other kids are doing.

Then I hear something downstairs, maybe conversation? I put my ear to the cool hardwood floor and strain to listen. All I hear is the sound of some game on David's laptop. Then the swish that comes when my mom rolls over to face the wall.

I leave the application half blank and go downstairs, nail polish in hand. This is what I do when I don't know what to do. I do stupid little things that are supposed to make people feel better. I give hugs; I give manicures. I try to figure out for just how many seconds a stunning shade of red will make her forget.

— Alyssa Woods

The Trouble with Gravity

I. The Mirror Farm

I grew up on my grandfather's mirror farm, a shimmering field of glass and aluminum always throwing sunlight in wandering angles. Every night, groping for sleep in the dark of the house, I could hear my grandfather stirring hot coals, smelting ores, tempering and pounding out long sheets of silvery alloy in the barn. He was forging the spine of each mirror — single steely vertebrae — from metal scraps that were delivered to the house once a week in wooden barrels.

Hammer and anvil, water and coal.

On sour summer days, restless and wet, I would go out to the field, the long reflective grid lying out in the sun. The mirrors stood so tall, absolutely flat, their beveled edges fitting together in sparkling walls flowing over the grass. It was so easy to get lost in there among the rows and columns of mirrors throwing switch-images at me, infusing my bones with prophecies of an inverse world. In a mirror, everything is a doppelgänger.

Lemon and platinum, emeralds and flesh.

As my grandfather grew older, he lost his steadiness of hand, causing him to leave traces of misplaced ripples and folds in the aluminum backing. That was when he first constructed fun-house mirrors, perverse contraptions in which I could make myself tall, slim, squat, or thick.

Over time, he replaced some of the flat-faced mirrors in the field with the distorted ones. Mistranscribed versions of me would stare back through waving windows, meandering through crunched glass, reaching out of crippled doorways in space. The reflections began to take on a certain individuality, separating their appearances from one another, one cell at a time. Sameness dissolved.

I multiplied myself in the grid. Mirror times mirror divided by self equals infinite skin.

Always face-shifting mockeries, leading me in spirals.

II. Flying Machine

I flew my car into a monstrous tree yesterday, but it really wasn't my fault. I was only trying to adjust the driver's seat's lower lumbar support when that ditch snuck up on me and catapulted my car into a low-hanging branch.

I flew like an armless pilot, or a kiwi bird. All the grace of a winged pig.

"Just my luck," I thought out loud, sitting in the car with the two rear wheels swallowed up in the mud, front dangling awkwardly from the gnarled oak. I bet this never happened to da Vinci, Gutenberg, or Einstein.

Leaf-litter and acorns, shaken from their places, crowded my windshield, framing a mist-veiled view of a cemetery in the distance. Each gloomy granite headstone just stood there, looming magnificently untouchable on its dark plot. I wanted to puke.

As I crawled down out of the door, I turned around to the street and saw the traffic slowing down — all the curious strangers riding by, rolling down their windows, snaking out loose-fitting Rubbermaid necks to see my broken flying machine in the tree. All the bug-eyed giraffe-people asked me was I okay. Just so they wouldn't look conspicuous or anything.

I'm doing great, I thought. Fantastic, thanks. My car is in a tree; I do this every day.

Even the little hang-ups — cars in trees, and all — make me lose my nerve.

I stood back and admired the boxy Ford Explorer in all of its shimmering onyx glory, suspended from the fat-bottomed oak. Untouchable. I could almost feel my head unscrewing itself from its fixture on my shoulders, hopping along the northbound shoulder of Ferns Crossing Road. Bizarre.

I needed to detach.

So I climbed the tree, branch by branch, until I could touch the sky. As I surveyed the cityscape sprawled out below, everything so falsely complete, I felt a raindrop lick my arm. Tiny beads dripped to the ground below, saturated the grass, shattered the silence untouchably.

The whole sky growled, softly rippling through the thunderheads, the air, the tree, my flesh. I looked up at the perfect yellow lemon spinning across the sky like a child's top in flight.

The sun split open, and I jumped.

III. On the Death of a Canadian Goose

5:18 A.M.: The whole world is asleep, swimming in the mouth of silence.

A single goose flies overhead, towing the morning sun in on its back. Right away I know that there is another one, dead, beside a road or in a field somewhere.

Geese always travel in twos apart from their arrowhead formations; they know there is strength in numbers. If one goose ever becomes sick or physically unable to keep pace with the rest,

11

another one will drop out of line and fly ahead of it to draft its wings to the ground, ease flight.

Geese on the ground are a gaggle; against the sky they are a flock.

When they land, the healthy goose mothers its companion, ever watchful. It serves as the eyes, ears, tendons of the other, snaking out of its windblown skeleton. They hold tightly together, hopeful and close, until they are both well enough to fly, or until death finds them in their sleep. Too often, only one bird flutters off to find the flock.

Feathers fall like thoughts upon the water.

A nasal honk peels back the early morning silence, and the goose flies overhead, cruising along the horizon, looking only for friends, and a way home.

Godspeed, friend.

— David Brothers

Falling

The question is always the same,
no matter how extreme or
casual; as long as there is
some sort of height (spiral staircase,
Juliet's balcony, a human pyramid),
you ask yourself,
What would happen if I fell?
We are inclined to think morbidly.
We love to imagine our funeral procession
and our first-grade teacher's response
when flipping through the obituaries: "She was
such a *good* girl."
And for three seconds you want to feel
the release, the intimacy with God
that psalms and incense
can't give you,
and you tell yourself that if you did it —
and now you are really tempted —
you would fall backwards
so you could look up.

— Maggie Johnston

Balzac in Bronze

My first sexual experience
came in Philadelphia — me
alone with Rodin's colossal
Balzac in bronze —
no cameras, security guards,
little girls, fathers with maps to catch me jam
my nails into Balzac's gutted
eye sockets, and wiggle — dig
the stone — then grab his lifeless hair,
thrust it against my chest,
press my nose to his furrowed brow.
      Balzac, lips pursed, feels no passion.
In my ecstasy, I see Victor Hugo frowning.

— Eric Linsker

I Didn't Know

We would sit on the Spanish Steps until our lips were swollen and chapped, until our tongues were coated with the taste of cigarettes, until our skin had melted and darkened from the heat of the sun. We would sit there wanting to be older, or at least look older, assuming everyone was staring at us, assuming everyone wanted us. We wanted our lives to advance, but we didn't know in what direction. We would wait, patiently watching the baggy pants boys, as we called them. They were such a rarity in Italy that when you found one you had to hang on. The baggy pants boys also consisted of leather-, chain-, and spike-wearing punks, tie-dyed hippies, and fifty-year-old drug addicts. They had a designated corner where they would all meet and disturb the peace while policemen hid around corners watching from afar. Every day we went there we would move closer and closer to their corner. We were spiders, and they were insects trapped in our web.

I had never seen Gian Luka there before. I figured he was new, so I let my cigarette dangle from my fingers as if offering something, as if telling him that everything I had was there for the taking. I didn't think I was enough for him. I didn't think I was enough for anyone. I liked his deep dimples, messy hair, and *I don't care* attitude. I wanted him. I wanted him to want me. We all had a designated baggy pants boy who we would watch like a dog begging for food at the dinner table. Our heads cocked, our eyes open, longing. We wanted them, not knowing what we wanted. He asked me if I would help him with something, would I come with him? I said yes, putting one weak foot in front of the other, hoping *help* didn't mean far away, hoping *help* didn't take place in a bedroom. He led me down the Spanish Steps and around the corner. I followed his shadow, not him. I was afraid of him. We stopped at a soiled public bathroom, and he told me to wait there as he knelt on the stairs below me. He told me to tell him if someone was coming, as he took out a coffee can and began putting its contents into plastic bags. "Drugs," he said. "But not really. I mean, this is just herbs and wood 'n' shit. But we sell it to the tourists 'cause they think it's drugs." He started up the steps, and along the way back he kept singing a line from a song that went "Don't worry, be happy." But when he sang it with his Italian accent, it sounded more like "Done wary, be 'appy."

"Let's go for a walk," he said, taking me to a back alley where we sat on a doorstep, speaking in two different languages, not understanding each other. Silence prevailed. And then he grabbed me, sticking his tongue down my throat, jamming it between my teeth, folding my tongue like laundry. I could taste the beer as his saliva collided with mine. I didn't know if I liked it. It was my first kiss. I didn't know.

He took me farther down the alley and leaned me up against a cold stone wall, my left leg rapidly shaking when he fingered my stomach, when he undid each button on my gray pants quietly, as if what he was doing was a secret, or wrong. My shirt climbed my stomach and I could feel the stones become part of the small of my back. My left leg shook faster, each time springing my knee forward, and I thought about how I could flee. I planned out each step in my mind as he touched me. I saw my knee spring forward, hitting him in his crotch and running. I saw myself underwater, clean and cold, wrapped in a blanket of seaweed. He touched me like I was a Popsicle on a hot summer day,

16

and he had to touch every inch of my body before I melted. When he reached the last button, he asked me if I'd ever had sex before. "Yes," I said. I thought if I said yes it would make it easier to say no. I don't know what my reasoning was, but I didn't want him to realize that I wasn't enough. "Do you want to have sex?" he asked. "No," I murmured apologetically, then added, " 'cause, I mean, my friends are waiting for me." As if I had to have an excuse, as if I had to explain why I wasn't ready. I remember the padded bra I wore. I remember worrying if I had put on enough deodorant. Then I began to worry if I had put on any deodorant at all. He slid his finger along the top of my underwear, the underwear my mom had bought two sizes too big. The underwear lined with black lace and black bows. The underwear I had gotten when I had my first period. He exhaled into my ear, and I could feel my eardrums beat against his breath, wanting to burst free, to escape. He placed his hands on my waist and drew them toward the fly of my pants. I can still see him sliding each button through its hole. In black and white, in slow motion, in disappointment. I wasn't enough. And I knew it. During my walk home I kept pushing piece after piece of gum into every region of my mouth. I chewed rapidly, trying to get rid of the taste of his tongue and leftover saliva.

My friends screamed and bubbled in excitement at our first contact with the baggy pants boys. I thought I was happy. I hoped I was happy.

"Did you like it?"

"Don't you think it was a little quick to let him touch you the night you met him?"

"Was it fun?"

"Does he know you're a virgin?"

My friends filled my room with curiosity as we lay on the floor. They didn't really care what the answer was. They already had their own visions of what had happened.

I lay there, crossing my legs and squeezing my thighs together. I didn't want to go back the next day, even though I knew I should, even though I knew I would. I hated the fact that he had touched me, I hated myself for letting him touch me. And I hated the fact that I had disappointed him, and that I wasn't enough. I perceived his touching me as a compliment. I never thought someone would want to touch me. I never reckoned someone would, at least not for a long time. I didn't like the smell of his breath. I didn't like the temperature of his body, or the texture of his skin. I didn't like him touching me. I didn't like him wanting me because I didn't want myself. I clasped my thighs together and wished they would become stuck like that forever. I still didn't know what I wanted, but I knew I didn't want him. I didn't like my mouth being invaded, my eyes searched or body groped. I didn't like my breath smelled, my voice heard, or my ears whispered to. I didn't know I wouldn't like any of it. It was my first kiss, my first touch. I didn't know what I wanted. I didn't know.

We went back the next day. And the next day. And during the two weeks after my first kiss, we went there every day. We met his friends. Orso (meaning bear), Giallo (meaning yellow), Pizello (meaning small penis), Diego, Matteo, and Carmello. Orso was roughly 275 pounds. Beady eyes that stalked you behind glasses that pinched the fat on either side of his face, squeezing sweat from his skin like pulp from an orange. He would pull me onto his lap and bounce me, the fat jiggling in his legs, like I was sitting in a bowl of Jell-O. He would press his goatee upon the back of my neck and rub it up and down, up and down, up and down. His bristly hairs stinging my flesh, the smell of ham on his breath. I didn't like his hairs on my neck, I didn't like sitting on his lap or the scent of ham. I didn't like him. They called me their doll, but I didn't mind. It made me feel good that they wanted me. One night as I was lying on the steps, Gian Luka appeared above me.

"Come on," he said. "Why are you doing this to me? Let's go for a walk."

"No." I giggled, pretending to be ignorant of the fact that he was so serious. His dry hands moved up and down my arms, casting flakes of my sunburned skin upon the stone steps.

"Please," he pleaded, while some of his friends stood behind him watching, telling me to do it, to go with him. I imagined the stones again. I imagined him moving up and down on top of me like the ebb and flow of the ocean. I imagined him being inside me, and I hated myself. I hated myself because I didn't want to have sex, because I wasn't ready. How could I let someone else in while I was trying to get out? I knew I was going to have to disappoint him. I stood up delicately, trying to seem as if I were enjoying myself, as if I were having a good time. As if I were still six, and I giggled at the word *sex*, thinking it was a secret game.

An acquaintance of ours, Lily, came along the next day. She was from Milan and wanted to see Rome. So we brought her to the Spanish Steps. He didn't say hello. He made it clear he didn't care that I was there. He was shirtless and drunk at three in the afternoon. Beer glistened on his bottom lip like dewdrops on flower petals. He looked Lily up and down and leaned against a wall, complimenting her loudly. "Anna — you see this? You

19

should get your belly button pierced like this. And you should get your nose pierced." I said okay, propping my hand on my forehead, the sun beating down upon my back. It was beating a migraine into my head. Gian Luka turned his back against me. Lily told us to get together for a picture as Gian Luka leaned into her. I knew she was preparing me, apologizing for what would follow later in the evening.

He came and sat next to me, smiling, with his eyes rolled up in his head.

"Kiss!" she said. "Anna, smile!" So we did. We pressed our lips together. *It's just skin*, I thought. I didn't want to kiss him, but I thought that if I could convince him I still wanted him, then maybe he would stay with me. If I could convince him there might be a chance of me letting him in, of me giving myself up to him, maybe I wouldn't be such a disappointment. I kept asking myself, why won't I let him fuck me? It's nothing but skin made up of organisms and tissue and stuff. It's nothing but a body. My body.

He asked Lily to go on a tour of Rome with him. She said yes, looking at me with an apologetic look on her face, handing me the picture. I knew what that tour would consist of — a bedroom maybe, most likely an alley. He winked at me like we were best buds and he was about to score big-time. My friends tried to stand in front of me. They tried to prevent me from seeing. But I knew. I ran my tongue along the inside of my mouth and tried to forget the feeling of his teeth on my lower lip and his hands clinging to my waist. I heard the English language as it surrounded me, tourists commenting on the Spanish Steps, closing in on me, suffocating me. I waited for him to return. I didn't know why.

He fucked her three times that afternoon. He fucked her earrings from her ears, he told me, as if pointing out what I had missed. The opportunity of a lifetime. He was telling this to me while I smiled, pretending to be listening to another conversation. But no one else was talking. "I gotta go," he said to me, his friend. "My girl is waiting for dessert." He placed his hands on my knees. "Ciao," he whispered pityingly, extending his neck toward mine in expectation of a kiss. I turned my head and kissed his cheek. I almost said thank you. But he was already gone.

He never got to see my belly button pierced, or a stud in my nose. He never got to see my red, purple, blue, orange, brown, black, or green hair. He never got to see how hard I tried to be enough. I never learned how to say no. I didn't know I would ever have to. I was thirteen years old. It was my first kiss. I didn't know I wouldn't like it. I didn't know what he would want. I didn't know, and I still don't. I continue to lie at night squeezing my thighs together, gazing at the picture of our lips pressed together, taped above my bed, dreaming of days where I may be enough.

— Hanna Zipes

Eulogy for John Berryman

Mother found him in the living room,
when she went to draw the curtains.

She passed the couch to find him
crumpled there like a soggy grain sack.
It was such a surprise to see
the insomniac resting that, at first,
she didn't notice the wrinkled wet skin
of his hands, the slip of a rope around his neck.

His dead-eyed stare froze her;
blood rushed from her cheeks.

Taking up the knife beside him,
she sawed off the sleeve of his blazer
and draped it over his face like a veil.

His wide-eyed stare had accused her
of thievery, she said,
"of clutching at others' lives."

I won't go near the room.

— Brittany Cavallaro

Always

Sometimes I find boys
and I want to
run my fingers
through their hair
kissing their neck

Sometimes I find boys
that I slip
into crushes with
They always smell like soap
They always like other boys

— Mary Brady

Left of Center

I'm so shy
my cat has started
attending parties for me.
He went
to a botanical soiree
last night, brought me back
some petits fours,
a glass of white wine,
and a still-bleeding meadowlark.
I am told
he makes effortless small talk.

Maybe I
was supposed to start this way,
poetically:
I should wear white in October,
spit gum off the town's highest building,
speak in cryptic haiku.
Or maybe
I'll live as a hermit,
respectably,
and only make pilgrimage for Wheatabix.

Perhaps
an isolation booth is my calling —
I'll work in the cemetery,

steal food, leave
my party dresses unironed.
Can't society
always use another freak?
Enough time with pondering —
I have to go
sweep the porch,
let my cat out
to wander our back-alley dumpsters.

It's what he was meant for,
after all.
He never looked good
in dress shoes.

— Mia Osborn

Matricide

My mother is a television set.

I run my fingers over the dust that settled on her screen like dry dew; her glass is cold and inert; all warmth and life have left her. It's been a week since I turned her off, and I have not yet succumbed. I haven't come crawling back, fingertips tiptoeing over the rubber buttons of the remote, telling myself, "Don't turn her on. Don't turn her on." Her power button has not known the green of its bulb in a week, and I have no urge to bring her back.

When she deserves it, I unplug her, but usually only for a few days. Afraid of what might happen if I left her off too long, whether her ghost would go cold in the tubing, whether she would curl like smoke through the circuitry, spiral out the cord and through the socket, and drift through a million transmissions, I would turn on the TV to forgive her and only see the blank stares of actors and the profound silence of dialogue.

At this point, I don't even care.

We didn't used to be like this. We fought less when we were first developing a system of communication. She knew the pulse of every program. If she wanted to speak, she constructed a syntactic collage. She skimmed every channel in an electric blur until she found the show she wanted. "Hello," Lucille Ball would say, and Mom would leapfrog through programs and have a detective say my name: "Sara."

In this way my mother's voice was the mimicry of a million men and women. Her face was the bored blur of flipping channels.

Her laughter was the canned laughter of sitcoms. There was applause in her laughter.

It was cold and impersonal, but we rarely fought. One time we did, and I sat patiently in the dark with a bowl of cereal while my mother flipped through every channel in search of forgiveness. Even during our most violent disagreements, the idea of unplugging her was a joke, a taboo.

"What if I *did* stay out past curfew?" I asked her, cereal milk dribbling down my chin. "Flip to a channel of someone spanking their daughter?"

I waited while she thumbed through her lexicon, piecing "Tell . . . your . . . father" together from the spare sentences of random channels.

Dad was the night watchman at our local bookstore. He sat in a closet-size room with a wall of security monitors, watching the black-and-white surveillance tapes, the color-sucked ghosts of customers moving through grainy film. He burned his eyes out on monochrome and came home to watch his wife. She flickered across his exhausted face.

He paid the electric bills necessary to keep Mother constant. He was lonely. He and Mom talked, but mostly he watched TV and she kept silent. Or he put a movie in the VCR and she became car crashes and explosions. More than once my father obscured Mom with videotapes and, when he thought no one was watching, began weeping.

Late one night, awoken by a noise, I stumbled noiselessly into the living room and caught my father masturbating; he didn't see me, but I spied for a minute. Curiosity and horror kept me there.

Mom had switched to an adult film and watched as he made love to her. He jerked slowly and deliberately while men came in Mom's face. He yawned. Guilt kept him from coming; he struggled, punishing himself to orgasm in quick bursts of fervent pumping, but nothing. Defeated by the lonely obligation of intercourse, he moved to turn her off, a lonely erection wilting in his boxers. He picked up the remote and turned her off; she turned herself back on with a hum. Dad sighed and sat there, and I went back to sleep.

"Tell your father," she had said.

"You can't tell Dad if I unplug you," I had threatened with a grin on my face. It was preposterous, an empty threat. I wouldn't unplug her. I was the girl who broke down during every brownout, who was racked with sobs every time the power stuttered, who rushed to see if my mother was still there, still breathing in the tubing.

She jumped to some maudlin TV movie about a cancer-ridden father. The doctor told the son, "Pull the plug." It was a dare, a showdown. She laughed with me. She laughed the laughter of a live studio audience.

I did unplug her. A spark jumped when her prongs left the socket.

I had come home late one night. I was drunk. I stumbled into the living room. Mother cast blue shadows across the carpet. She had been talking to herself. "But no man's ever made that passage!" she muttered softly. My mother was an amateur pilot in a made-for-TV movie saying his prayers in the cockpit. My mother dipped and rolled and won the war. She derived some satisfaction from this, I think.

I collapsed onto the couch. "Mom?" A slurred whisper. A drunk whisper.

I listened to the clicking of my mother in search of a message. Millisecond cuts of sound, stuttered vowels. She stopped on some weepy TV movie about an abusive alcoholic beating his wife. "Shut up, you drunk *bastard*!" my mother screamed through dramatic, overacted tears.

I just stared at the screen.

"You stupid bitch," the man rejoined. I knew my mother wasn't drunk; she *couldn't* drink, but in choosing the words of a drunk, it was the same. It was as close as I could get to coming home and seeing her nursing the puddle at the bottom of a wineglass and yelling at me. Beer-ushered tears welled.

I was near sobbing, and my voice broke when I whispered, "You're drunk."

She found the face of a man staring deeply into the camera.

"Mom, I can explain. Trevor and I —"

She pounced upon this new information, this realization that I was drunk and had been alone with a boy, and my mother became a lesbian in an adult film, telling her partner, telling *me*, "You're a dirty *slut*."

And if my mother could slap, if my mom could pull hair or had hair to pull, I might never have unplugged her. We would have become one through fingernails and teeth and tangled hair entwined around our fists. I threw pillows at her, and her audiences laughed, and I screamed, ripped at my hair. She wouldn't stop laughing, so I beat the top of her with my palm flat, her image jumping on the screen. Snot and tears made mingled streams around my mouth. The audience mocked me.

Afraid to unplug her electric cord, I reduced her to basic cable. She began screaming static.

Fifty channels gone, my mother became the snow crash of a million black-and-white ants scurrying over themselves. My mother's voice became white noise. She cast light, white fire on the walls. She pushed the volume bar to her limit, and she screamed static as loud as she could; it was deafening, all the rage and betrayal and hatred reduced to a gargling hiss.

She hit the major stations, looking for the right words. Her dictionary had been crippled, and she had to wait. It took her ten minutes to pilfer words from the weathermen and police officers to construct the sentence. I waited for her to finish while trying to control my breathing on the carpet:

"I . . . have . . . no . . . daughter."

Too tired to scream, too exhausted to keep hitting her, to fling any more pillows across the room, I muted her. I tore my mother's tongue out. Her mouths moved without sound. A woman screamed at the top of her lungs, *Psycho*. My mother's veins swelled in her throat, her hair was matted, her face dirty and cut. She screamed as loud as she could, and no sound came out.

So I unplugged her.

I ripped her from the wall. My mother became a supernova in reverse, every image reduced to a white core in her center, a bright star glowing and humming for half a second before leaving the room in complete darkness, a white star in her face, a bullet hole.

But she wasn't dead. At two in the morning, I heard Dad come in and turn her on. Heard the weather report, the news, an infomercial, and some old sitcoms as they spoke. She could not be killed.

After I saw that the supernova was harmless, unplugging her became less of a struggle. I still tried to avoid doing it, on principle, finding other ways to punish her. When she cheated on my father, becoming emotionally attached to some actor and following him from station to station, watching his show and its reruns, waiting for his face in commercials and kissing him with his lips projected against her glass mouth, his body translated into electric signals and pulsing through her tubing, I muted her and left the room. I let her captions move pointlessly in a vain and voiceless march. I took the remote and turned the channel while she tried to explain, cutting her off midsentence. With the frustration of a stammerer, she tried to bleat curses through truncated words. I precipitated her impediment until she grew ashamed of her stutter and sat in silence. I videotaped her and stowed her in the attic, imprisoning her in celluloid. I muted her and made her watch, paralyzed, as Trevor ravaged me on the couch, as I got high, as I burned photographs of her.

But these humiliations weren't enough, and it wasn't long before pulling the plug became second nature.

I have killed her a hundred times.

The voice in the screen is different every time I turn her back on. I wonder if Mom died a year ago, the first time I turned her off, if the woman who has been haunting the Magnavox is just another ghost in the shell, if I have sifted through a hundred mothers throughout my adolescence.

But I don't bother myself with it.

She's off right now, and I run my fingertips over her screen.

Dad's up north for a funeral, and I've been increasing the increments I keep my mother adrift in the tubing. I've been seeing how long I can hold her under before she comes sputtering up for breath in a burst of static or stops breathing altogether. She's been under and inert for a week now. Her screen is cold.

I press the power button.

There is a blue and bloated corpse bobbing in a river. Some policemen point at her and nod, spitting chaw into the bushes.

My mother is death and resurrection and shampoo commercials. My mother cannot be killed.

— Bennett Sims

Rehoboth, Summer 1992

The waves on a summer night
are drawn again and again
like angry lovers to crash against the shore
they can neither conquer nor forget.
The small, silver pearl of the moon
floats on a dark wind
above the brooding sea.

They say the moon controls the tides,
but is it the moon that roils the waves
or a storm far out at sea?
Hurricanes are born in Africa.
They carry the heat of deserts,
the heavy scent of exotic flowers
and sweet, lush fruits we have never seen.

I stand at the water's edge.
Cool waves froth around my ankles.
Sand, still warm from the sun,
slides away beneath bare toes.
I throw back my head and breathe
the wind, but only the tart, familiar
scent of salt tickles my nose.

— Elisabeth Gorey

Liturgical Procession

Freya's brother likes to tell stories in which he's a rebel. He tells them in a disjointed way whenever something sparks his memory. He always starts in the middle, like he's just resuming an earlier conversation.

"I still can't believe we did that," he says on Friday afternoon as they make dinner in the kitchen. He laughs a bit and looks up from turning the crank on the pasta machine. Today is pierogi day, and the two are making them in the only way they can be made right: slowly, with methodical care. It is a listening food to make, the type of thing that takes two people the whole afternoon to prepare. Before Alek runs the rest of the dough through the machine, he turns to Freya. "It was winter, you know," he says, as if that will shed light on the subject.

"Winter?" she asks. Her voice is not impatient, just a little questioning. Alek is often unintentionally obscure, and she frequently needs to lead him through stories. It doesn't drive her crazy, though. This is just one of the things she is used to about her brother.

"In Warsaw," he says, as if that makes it clearer. Freya glances at the TV on the kitchen counter. It is switched to the twenty-four-hour news channel. The woman behind the news desk is talking about the Pope, who is visiting Poland this week. The news program cuts to a video clip of the Pope being wheeled through a crowd of worshipers. Some of them are cheering. Freya knows that she should know what they're saying, but she doesn't. She wishes they would say *please*, or *thank you*, or maybe one of the numbers from one to twenty. If the churchgoers were saying those things, she'd be able to cheer along with them.

"Well?" she says. Her voice is casual, but she wants him to continue. Most of his stories are set in the pre-American years, most of which are also pre-Freya years. Their family left Poland when she was only a few months old, and so the stories her older brother tells are bittersweet, but as necessary for her to hear as the stories she has lived out herself.

"When the Pope came," he says.

"Oh, yeah," she says, and takes the dough Alek has just finished running through the pasta maker and lays it flat. She knows this story well. He knows this, but tells it anyway, and she listens.

"The Pope was in Warsaw," he says, "and we were all really excited. It was rare, you know, that he could visit. Everything was still Communist." He feeds fresh dough into the pasta machine and turns the crank. "This is before you were born, and Mama wanted to get her belly blessed with you in it, so that you would be a healthy, good child."

Freya smiles as she cuts the dough into circles using an old glass. It is a habit of Alek's to include her as much as possible in his stories of Poland, even ones that took place long before her time. He says *a few years before you were conceived*, or *when there was still only me and Elzbieta*. This helps Freya believe that the family was incomplete before she was born. Even as adults, they keep the old pattern: She worries about her alienation from her family or birth country, and he tries to alleviate her fears. She is grateful for his reassurance.

"So, we walked to the cathedral near the center of the city," he says. "You know which one?" Perhaps it is his creative story-telling, but sometimes he seems to forget that Freya has absolutely no memory of Poland.

"Maybe," she says, pressing the pierogi closed with the tines of a fork. There is no use in saying no.

Her noncommittal answer satisfies him, so he continues telling the story. "By this point, Papa was already here in the States, so Mama was on her own, trying to keep track of Elzbieta and me. I didn't exactly make that easy for her." Alek laughs, and uses the glass to cut circles from the dough, even though Freya has not finished stuffing the circles she already has. "I was eleven, so of course I had other plans."

Freya stuffs another pierogi, then sets the fork down on the table. She looks at Alek intently. Maybe her memory is faulty, but she cannot remember a time when he had any plan. In her early memories of him, he is a teenager with little direction, and then a college student without a major. The sequence progressed, and now he is a divorcé in his late thirties who cooks with his sister on Fridays. In Alek's stories, though, he always has a plan. Freya wonders whether this is something that he lost in time.

"I found my friend Jacek," Alek says as he stuffs and seals a pierogi, "and we shoved our way to the front of the crowd lined along the procession route. The day before we'd been making spitballs and firing them at people on the street, and Jacek still had the straws, so he handed me one and some paper from his pocket, and we started the game again. Things like ten points to hit a woman's purse and twenty to hit a priest's shoes." Alek places the finished pierogi on a pan. "So the procession starts — all of the priests in the city, and the higher-up clergy, too — and soon enough, the Pope came into sight, with a bishop walking on either side of him. Everyone around us started cheering and Jacek didn't even bother to whisper when he said to me, 'A hundred points for the cross on one of those bishops' hats.'" Alek grins. "You know what I mean?"

"Yeah, I do," Freya says, smiling as well. They have made so many pierogi that she is starting a new pan.

"So I made the spitball," Alek says, "but I was so nervous and excited that I spat too much. I fired it, and *bull's-eye*" — he slaps his hands together, sending a cloud of flour into the air — "it hit right in the center of a bishop's cross. The thing is, though, the guy was so tiny that where the spitball hit was about the height of the Pope's forehead, and some of the spit grazed him. So the Pope actually stops in the middle of the procession and gives me and Jacek this look without even rubbing his face off. And I still had the straw in my mouth and everything." It is easy to tell he enjoys remembering the appalled look on John Paul II's face when he got hit with spitball residue.

"So," Alek says, "it's not like the whole crowd got quiet or anything, but there was kind of a hush. After a second, the procession started again. We were about to run, but right then Jacek's father grabbed us and pulled us out of the crowd." Alek winces as he opens the oven door to put the trays of pierogi in. "Not only did Jacek's father make it so that neither of us could sit down for two weeks, but the priest assigned us two hundred and fifty Hail Marys."

"Yeah?" Freya says.

"Yeah." He closes the oven door and leans back against the counter. "But it was worth it." Alek's smile fades, and Freya notices that in the afternoon light he looks old, much older than she's ever seen him. "Yeah," he says again, his eyes following the Pope on-screen. His voice is unsure. "It was worth it."

— Elizabeth Szypulski

A Question of Music

I. Vexations

The haunting strains of Erik Satie's *Vexations* echo throughout the chapel. At five forty-five in the morning a heavyset woman slouches at the piano with her eyes glued to the single sheet of music. Three college students comprise the entirety of her audience, their sleeping bags stretching lengthwise across the pews. When I walk past they don't stir.

What compels the woman to continue playing, even when it is obvious that no one is listening? An all-night vigil, or perhaps martyrdom for some heroic cause? The actual meaning behind her stoicism seems much less valiant to me — the piece is simply not yet completed. We still have fifteen hours left.

She doesn't budge until the clock rolls to six o'clock and I slink into her position just as she stands up. As my fingers smoothly replace hers on the keyboard, I try to behave as seriously as she did, but I can't help sneaking a look every now and then toward the pews. An unprofessional move, surely, but I am too sleepy to care. From my vantage point, it appears as though the church is empty. I have no audience, but still I continue to play.

II. Satie's intentions

"To play this motive eight hundred and forty times continuously, it would be good to prepare previously, and in the most lengthy silence, motionlessly and somberly." The longest piece of music ever written consists of only two lines of notation and the aforementioned instructions. At fifty-two beats per minute, a complete performance of the *Vexations* lasts exactly twenty-eight hours. Though the piece is built around only eighteen chords, the transmutation of accidentals makes it nearly impossible to memorize. Thus, after every two-minute repetition, the performer must read the music with new eyes. Satie wanted his piece to have a unique psychological effect on both the performer and the listener, and to test the boundaries of music as we know it.

III. Audience

After four hours of playing background music in the refrigerated section of Thriftway, my teeth chattered uncontrollably and my lower back was beginning to ache. They had hired me to create a classy atmosphere for their wine tasting, but so far all I'd cooked up were some quizzical looks and a few curious toddlers who never knew how close was too close when running their sticky hands over my piano bench.

One man, who had obviously had far too many samples of chardonnay, plopped himself down next to me and began expounding nostalgically about his days as a rock musician. "We used to go down to my basement and play like this!" he exclaimed, banging on my piano with his clenched fists. "Okay," I said with a smile, and then continued to play my Beethoven sonata. For the next twenty minutes he insisted on holding my music open for me, turning the pages at random intervals and loudly wishing for his youthful days in the music industry.

Stationed behind me was the man selling Aunt Margaret's Marionberry Cheesecakes™. By the fourth hour, I knew every detail of his dear auntie's cheesecake-making skills. In fact, I could have given the spiel myself, except I would have cut out the section where his auntie runs out of milk and races out to her neighbor's barn to milk the cow herself. Though he forced himself onto every passing customer, he never so much as offered me a sample. In the end we had built a lovely relationship in which he requested a pop song from the sixties, and I replied that I had never heard of it. We managed to carry on this dialogue for quite some time before he realized I was never going to play one of his songs.

IV. Challenge

There is an innate joy in learning to play a piece of music with confidence. After the first few weeks, the notes on the page become friendly and well known, and the first strides are made toward building our beautiful relationship. In the next step, I find the broad strokes of style. The clearest melody or offset harmony is selected and raised above the undercurrents, patterns of dynamics are selected and implemented, articulations are defined.

Then comes the hard work — tearing apart each phrase note by note, cluster by cluster, searching for the underlying pattern. Small themes are discovered with joy, like when a detective solves a mystery. I experiment with the breath of the passage, the softness of each fingertip, the bite with which each muscle is working to bed the key. Hours of daily practice aim toward fitting the final product into the curve of my hand. I play each section at triple speed, half speed, varying the rhythms, deconstructing and analyzing each series of notes until I can see and feel the tactile image of my hand moving into the keys exactly as I envision them. Then performance and the ineffable throes of success. The enemy is conquered, the lover is embraced.

V. Vexations

Forty-five minutes into my performance of the *Vexations*, the repeating chords begin to take on a lulling, hypnotic quality. I am completely bored; no wonder my audience is asleep. I wonder what would happen if I suddenly stopped playing, or — worse yet — if I started to play "Happy Birthday." I am certain that the earth would shake and the students would awaken; the spell would be broken and the clouds would lift from their eyes. Instead I continue plodding along with my performance, my only competition their noisy snoring.

The music itself is one of the most maddening things I've ever seen. There is no obvious pattern, no melody to cling to, no rhythmic pattern to grasp. The tempo must be kept exactly even, and the dynamic markings are strictly maintained at a soft rumbling. The slowness of each successive chord serves to tie the beginning to the end, creating even more of a cyclical momentum to the piece. Each time I began a new repetition, my hand had to learn the chords anew. I was never allowed to own the piece. We remained strangers for the entire sixty minutes, never permitting so much as a peek into our combined interests.

VI. Competition

Rules for Competition: Always memorize your piece, but bring a copy of your music, freshly erased of all pencil markings, for the adjudicator. Number the measures. If your hands are cold, bring mittens. Always adjust the height of the bench and lower the music rack before you begin. Bow before you play and after you play, regardless of whether or not someone is clapping. When bowing, keep your hands at your side and stand straight. Smile. Keep your fingernails clipped so short they bleed, or they will click when you play. Rest your hands on your lap before you play, and never stand up while your hands are still on the keyboard. No high heels, no fingernail polish, and no short skirts. Always play hungry.

In this manner, you are sure to look a professional and perform like a professional, which will skyrocket you above your competition, making you sure to win. Bring home your gold medal and stow it away where no one will see it.

VII. Aspirations

When my brother took the stage to solo with the Oregon Symphony, I was sure that I was clapping the hardest out of anyone in the audience. He was the headliner and the last performer, and as the crowd erupted in a standing ovation for his triumph over Rachmaninoff's second concerto, I swelled with happiness. I have always been excessively proud of my older brother and his monumental accomplishments.

I loved hearing stories about how he toured in Russia and was mobbed by adoring fans who demanded autographs, critics who wrote rave reviews in Cyrillic, television stations that followed him around with cameras and showed reruns of his interviews and concerts for weeks. My brother, the international piano phenom. At home he was nothing less than a local celebrity — performing for various charity events, winning prestigious competitions, earning invitations to distinguished banquets.

But during my own piano lessons, my teacher quickly grew frustrated with my comparative lack of talent. She chastised me for running track instead of putting in four hours of practice a day, especially when it meant I came to my lessons with hands ice-cold after a meet. I tried to come to piano class instead of studying math. I tried to write essays while practicing the piano. Neither compromise proved successful. My teacher expected that one day I would follow in my brother's footsteps, and I wanted to do so more than I ever let on.

My mother knew better. She told me to set my priorities straight, and if piano couldn't be at the top, to give up my lofty dreams. I cried when I realized she was right.

Nowadays I find myself accompanying my high school choir and soloing in department store lobbies. I will never be a famous concert pianist, I will never devote myself completely to my music, I will never be my brother. I am entirely someone else.

VIII. Tradition

Every year my family drives to Idaho for Thanksgiving. Idaho is where all of my mother's relatives live, though we always stop in The Dalles, which is where my father's relatives live. The sad truth is that my father's family thinks that Thanksgiving should consist of passing through the buffet at the Holiday Inn while carrying on boring conversations about the weather in a rather unfriendly fashion. My mother's side is quite the opposite — our get-togethers are always centered around good food and good company, so we make the seven-hour trek across Oregon every year. Flying takes only forty-five minutes, but it's so much better to drive. It's part of the tradition.

The rest of Thanksgiving is like a familiar dance. We pull into my grandparents' driveway well after midnight, but all of the relatives are awake and waiting for us with mountains of cold noodles to eat. The next morning we refuse to notice the one-hour time difference and wake up much later than we should, to find that Grandma has already started cooking the Thanksgiving feast. Food preparation is an all-day event.

We always have both a turkey and prime ribs, dozens of side dishes, and a pumpkin pie for dessert. For the next twenty-four hours we eat nothing but hot turkey sandwiches and leftover mashed potatoes. When we can no longer bear the combination of gravy and Jell-O salad, we order takeout Chinese food.

On Sunday morning my family departs for Portland so we can make it home in time for school on Monday. As soon as the car hits the freeway, into the CD player goes the Christmas music. We effectively transform the season from Thanksgiving to Christmas with the push of a button. It is always sad to leave behind our favorite relatives and all those leftover goodies, but the familiar bells and choral strains of the music remind us that good things are still to come. The sweet songs of Christmas remain lodged in our cassette decks and our ears until December 26, when they are forcibly removed. After all, there must be something definitive to mark the end of a tradition, if only so you can reach for it again someday and still feel the thrill of delight as the next song begins.

IX. Vexations

After my requisite hour of vexing, a perky blond girl takes over my position at the keyboard. There is no applause, no recognition of my performance at all. No one in the audience has even known I was there. In my hour of playing those chords, I have not so much as inched toward self-expression or self-discovery. There is no postperformance euphoria in sight. After mulling over the oddities of the morning, I still can't decide why that marathon of boredom is considered music, and why exactly I had agreed to play. Satie's vexations have succeeded. I am utterly dumbfounded.

— Lori DesRochers

Nightly Wonderland

As I lie in bed
the light through the window
hits one of the walls
and makes it look like another doorway

The little girl in me
long since outgrown
wants to run to the secret passageway
and find my Wonderland, my Secret Garden,
find my own special place

But the teenager currently residing here
cynical without reason
knows that if I jump out of bed —
probably stub my toe in the process —
if I come to that wall
if I reach out my hand
I'll just be disappointed

— Natalie Wright

Oriental

you said i looked like the
Odalisque
and i thought that was beautiful
until i found that in Turkish
it meant
"harem slave girl"

and saw her horse hips,
serpentine arm reaching
too far,
holding a teasing
feathered fan of peacock

while the other leg
fumbles childlike and twisted
like a hobbling vestigial organ, yet
every inch voluptuous,
down to the provocative
turn of head.

maybe i should learn the mudras.
maybe i should burn the Kama Sutra in the street.

maybe then you would carve me out
of Ingres and cast me Judith
in a visceral Gentileschi.

— Margaret Wohl

This Cowboy

It was late enough in March for thick air to weigh down skin and hair. Smack in the center of town, the only movie theater was showing *Boys Don't Cry* — a film to shake up a white-bred, suburban town like this one, with its tame churches and Saturday lawn boys. The seven o'clock showing began four minutes late and ended in a silence as rich and white as bone, a silence that numbed all of me except a tiny, flitting secret.

Crunched between my parents, I watched. The movie spun tight circles of color and confusion in my mind as Teena Brandon transformed herself into Brandon Teena, a short-haired, somewhat scrawny man with a strategically placed sock in her pants — convincing enough to be a cowboy stud, lady-killer. I saw Brandon fall in love, get found out, raped, and murdered. I watched Brandon's every mannerism, memorizing them, knowing them as my own because somehow I had always had them. I had them every time I read *Huckleberry Finn*. I had them every time I lifted the plastic limbs of my G.I. Joes. And I had them every time I hopped a fence, ran faster than everyone in the race, watched a girl. From the first moment she appeared on-screen, Brandon talked to me. She talked into bone and blood, into the very nucleus of my psyche until the looming movie screen quivered and sparked into a bolt of pixels that shocked itself out into the audience, joining us into one sexually confused identity crisis who wanted to be a cowboy so bad she would spend the rest of her life breathing for it.

If I gripped the two cold, metal armrests, the shaking stopped. If I gripped hard enough, the thoughts stopped: the thoughts that were changing subconscious to conscious, and leaving the distinct residue of shame on my tongue. Disgusted with myself, horny with the magnitude of it all, I sat in the backseat and reviewed the last one hundred and eighteen minutes. I had seen a graphic lesbian love scene, a brutal rape, and two murders by pistol. I had seen brutality and hate in their ugliest forms, and deep within the marrow of it all, I had seen myself. But it wasn't really me, it was a cinematic ghost of me opening its big, hollow throat to swallow me down far enough to forget who I was, why my crotch is a crease and not a bulge, why my hips don't point to one magnificent joint but jiggle as they open wide, wide, wide. Far enough to forget why my collarbones look so small, because I am inside something so big, because under these collarbones is the destruction of any illusions I wanted intact. They fall useless to my breasts, my hands, and the sway of my hips, the way I could catch a man's eye and hold it as long as I wanted to, if I wanted to. Under those collarbones is something much more intimate than I ever want to give. I want hardness, solitude in maleness that no woman could ever achieve, not even my little hero, Brandon. A woman knows too much, thinks too much, preoccupies herself with possibilities and impossibilities too much. She is conscious of all things evil and all things martyrizing. She is aware of her place in the world as the complex one, the esoteric one. No woman can escape the backbreaking instinct, the unforgiving pledge to live compromised as the weaker sex.

The car sputtered and stopped at a house that must have been mine because my dad said, "Here we are." But I was deep, deep down inside lost. When my parents fell asleep, I tiptoed into the narrow hallway to the medicine cabinet, snatching an Ace bandage and tiptoeing again over antique floorboards back to my room. I unraveled the bandage and wrapped my breasts over and over, tighter and tighter until all I could feel was the blood swelling, pounding to get through to my wrapped-up ribs and nipples. I denied the pounding with invented testosterone that was as new to me as it was real.

Life as I know it began when I was thirteen. I was sitting in a movie theater in my little town, stuck between shoulders of parents who later would not mind informing me that they regretted it. They regret with their warm hearts and they regret with their worn fingers until all that I am shatters into a thousand shards too soft to cut them and I have to excuse myself from the table.

— Eliza Brown

Understanding the Stories

Down by the stream I set up a tent. I hang my clothes on a line between birch trees. I dig a shallow fire pit in the sand and line it with round rocks. The rocks are wet and slick but dry quickly in the sun. They lose all color dry. In the tent I roll out an old sleeping bag that smells like mildew and sweat. The smells fill the tent. I unzip the flaps and let air in through the mosquito netting. I hang a battery-operated lantern from the ceiling, where the two aluminum tent poles cross. I take out my books. I have packed tea, apples, and tomato soup. The pots are charcoal stained and smell like wood fires.

I come here to forget my name. Sometimes it only takes a day, or a long night when the forest is alive with sounds. It can take up to a week. There is no view here; the summit of a mountain would give my soul a soaring that it does not deserve, not now. I swim in the stream, watch for black bears at the edges of the woods, where berry bushes ramble into birch and beech. I lie on the bedrock bank when the sun is high and try to follow the twisting tunnels of red and yellow light on my inside eyelids. They move very fast after a while.

I tear out pages from my books and nail them to the trees. They catch the wind and sometimes whisper a word from the text though it is not in English and could never be written. As night falls and the forest becomes tight and dark I move in close to the tent. I light a fire and eat my soup, sipping hot tea steeped in water from the stream. I will not restock the fire, as this is wasteful. I watch it until only the coals look back, then wipe off my feet and enter the tent.

I am here for the books. This is how I understand them. I come here to forget things. I come here because I want to feel something in the language that you cannot get from a simple reading through. I sleep with the books tucked under me. I read them in my sleep. I have carried with me Emerson, a children's book set in Maine that my father once read, druid prayer poems, and studies of wolves. This trip I devote to old photos.

Every woman in them is beautiful. They are poised and graceful, and the light is calm and kind to their features. I wonder if I could develop such grace if I sat long enough. There is something about waiting for the flash that relaxes the sitter. They do not hold large smiles or stiff poses. They seem to have been sitting, sleeping, standing in that position for a very long time. Their postures are nearly signature, as a certain hairpiece or brooch. I have torn them out of a history book about the prostitutes of the Yukon gold rush. They are strong women, who could cross mountain ranges and handle money. They are the sort of women I would like to be.

I tell them their stories, walk from tree to tree and speak to them. I am far away from where I believe their ghosts might dwell, and they do not respond. I repeat the facts of their lives, stare into the black-and-white of their eyes. Drying the stream's water from my skin, I try to take them in.

There is always a first. I come to her again and again. In 1887, Dutch Kate set out for the Yukon Territory on her own initiative; no man took her up north. Before Canadian wives and nuns claimed to be the first in the Yukon, she was already there.

At Chilkoot Pass, in southern Alaska, where mountain ranges come together, she climbed like a man, in man's trousers and high boots and hat, carrying a pack. She looked down onto wild country, London's land, mountains and rapid rivers. In her photo she posed like a lady, head lifted up to something heavenly, the light of the flash caught in her pale eye.

The men who traveled with her to gold camps called her a whore in their journals but when they docked at a native village she locked herself in the ship's cabin and put on the hoopskirt and the whalebone corset and the dainty little shoes lost under layers of petticoats. She laid powder on the sun freckles and tan on her chin and nose and pulled up her hair like the women in the big cities. The white men then called her an "apparition of loveliness" and the native chief spread Dall sheep blankets all the way to his lodge. She walked the whole way without getting dirty. I don't think she would have minded. It was a kind gesture, but Kate knew she was no goddess.

For a summer she slept with the chief, walked the coastal village in her finery, then continued north toward the men who paid in gold dust and heavy nuggets. Left the smell of salted salmon and Indian dogs and traveled through the dwarf spruce and sweet tundra willows. Up in Fortymile Country it was cold eight months a year and Kate bought as many provisions as she could, keeping a camp of fifty men alive for a winter when the pass was snowed in and the forty-mile river frozen solid. I wonder if that was foresight or savvy. In the spring a rescue party found the camp well—and Kate with only ten more cans of beans remaining.

She was remembered by those men in everything they wrote — letters home, journals. They said she had a grip on the souls of men, those white shoulders and slightly parted lips. They said she was aloof. She knew how to make herself up. A good lesson.

A judge saved her picture, said that she made enough money to go to school and become a nurse. By that time, Dawson was a boomtown and there was a tram over Chilkoot Pass. The mining towns had moved south and no one wintered anymore.

I am drawn to her daring, to her bold flaunting of natural charms. She holds her body and throws back her white shoulders like she is the most beautiful woman in the world. Such confidence. This is what men are attracted to, after all — this radiating assurance that passes as strength. I lift my head up. A blue heron flies low, looking for the small brown pond up in a fold between the hills. I long for a frontier, where land is unclaimed and can stay that way.

Beside the tent of slender birch is the picture of Mae Field, extravagant, scandalous. I sit beneath her, peering up as if she were onstage. I feel the blackberry bushes tightening around the campsite. One day this place will be overrun with them. The bears will move through, dark fur catching on the brambles. Mae Field's lips are lifting in a smile. She could say anything. Maybe laugh a sarcastic laugh, spit. She is seated, but I close my eyes and in a black-and-white faded image she stands, swings her hips to get the blood moving, and throws a wink at the photographer.

Delicate gloves hold the butt of her cigarette. She blows a perfect smoke ring against the black backdrop. She is dressed for travel with those scandalous ankles showing under the fringe. It wasn't the gold, she said. Gold was like pebbles, for picking up and throwing around. It was what the gold could buy that mattered.

The woman who interviewed her couldn't believe that the frail old lady in front of her was once the Doll of Dawson. Mae wanted to dance. In Hot Springs, South Dakota, a promoter named Whiskey set her up at the theater. There she met Arthur. He took her north, honeymooning on the Klondike trail. She crossed Chilkoot Pass at midnight — late in the season, stair steps chipped into the ice, moonlight out on the tundra.

Eight miles out of Dawson, at Bear Creek, she "got a hammer and knocked the gold loose in the cut, caught it in a pan, and took it to town." Got rich quick.

When her steamer sank a mile offshore, she jumped from ice floe to ice floe holding another woman's baby. On the bank she persuaded the chief of the Mounties to let the women sleep in the police station that night — the men outside with the sled dogs. Goddamn boat, she said, I'm never going south again. Mae didn't leave Alaska after that.

But Arthur returned to the lower forty-eight — went back to the Dakotas and married a nice Protestant girl. Mae took to dancing, was brought to court for hanging her lacy lingerie to dry on the street, showed a bit of a leg and a big smile.

She fell in love with a man who took her out on his bicycle, riding along the coast, drunk. They built a cabin by the shore. She felt something was draining out of the town. Spring was wet; rain brought the smell of the distant cedar forests up to her door.

The gold dried up and newcomers came and asked questions, asked her to bring that hemline down a bit, keep the men away, clean up her language. After finishing a three-month sentence of hard labor on the trails, she quit, moved to Ketchikan, kept quiet. I imagine she sat as she did in the photo, casual, waiting for somewhere to go, rolling cigarettes, and remembering the farm in South Dakota. People didn't ask personal questions in the north, she said, not in those days.

56

There's no place now where you can be only a body and a pair of eyes. I want my movements to be as anonymous as the deer on their trails. A footprint perhaps but no pictures, nothing owed, eating, sleeping, getting by. I have learned more at this campsite by the bend in the brook than I have in a classroom. Things sink in, like rainwater down through the aquifer. Facts begin to mean something. You can close your eyes and picture yourself as an eagle, or a woman a hundred years ago. Shamans known for shape-shifting. In Gaul the goddess of horses loved a priest who became a wolf and stalked her herds on nights when there was no moon. I would like to look down at my hands and see sand falling away. I would like to learn how the killdeer steps.

We share strands of DNA with oaks and everyone's ancestors. Out here I feel those old mitochondria stirring toward the surface of my cells. One morning I may look into the smooth stream and see the face of a woman I do not know. Her history will be in me, in blood and bone, not language. No one will remember when I slip out and never return.

Far out in the forest I have tacked a picture that haunts me. I cannot tell her story because it was never recorded. Her face is serene, as I imagine a woman who spent many days by still water might be. All that is written on her photograph is *Morning*.

That's all. Nameless. She could have been screwing for three dollars or she could've been an actor, a dancer in "a Bevy of Beauties," one of the "Finest Formed Women in Klondike," whores in the lead roles of *Uncle Tom's Cabin*, and dancing after that. I worry that my imagination will make her into the character I want her to be: spitfire, trekker, smart, and fierce. But she could have been simple, forced into this job by poverty, even slavery.

Her eyes look back inside. The shadows that fall on her are very dark, fading at the edges into her skin. She was looking for a Klondike king. That's what they were all looking for. A man with money. They hoped that they were pretty enough and good enough in the sack and could clean up their act quick enough for him to marry them, move them south, build them a big home with carpets and walls that didn't let in ground squirrels and arctic drafts.

She worked in Lousetown, downtown Dawson, in 1899, spilling down into the bay, a city of tents and shacks. A city with a red-light heart, where the houses of ill repute were the only buildings built to last. The bay opened out into the Bering, and when the wind blew cold from Russia and the ice floes locked in, the city moved south like snow geese and the caribou herds.

Morning. That's all he wrote — the man from the night before who woke her and asked for a picture. She should be sleeping. Sleep from dawn till four, then start work again. A cycle like those of the owl and the nighthawk. Deep shadows around her eyes, the sun rising up through her little window. Hair down. At night she put it up, dressed like the women from the cities, the women all the miners remember, passing women in Chicago and Seattle and the farmwives in their finest clothes at the Fourth of July picnic. Eyes distant. She's been paid to act her part — it's time for the man to leave. She is too tired to try to look beautiful but she is, soft and honest. Morning and her nightgown is slipping off a white shoulder — that pale skin of old pictures. Working out of the back of cigar stores and saloons and cabins. The only women around. Morning and the light is kind to her, to the corners of her mouth and the soft skin under her jaw. She says nothing to me. I can't imagine she would come back to haunt Dawson. There is no passion in her posture, easy, tired, bored. I like to think that ghosts return to places of contentment, places that they never wanted to leave. An angry spirit seems irrational. There are many places of pain and fear in a life but few where a soul would like to sit, like a rounded boulder beneath a waterfall, for as long as such things remain.

I wonder how many people would like to return to a city apartment or busy block, if when these things are gone, the quiet plain will be filled with spirits. I would like to move a bit. At the very moment when the sun sits on the horizon at dusk and the forest is strange and painted in unfamiliar colors, I can see out over the hills as a bird might. I move on updrafts over the Connecticut, down along the Merrimack and White River, over Moosalock and Cube, Camel's Hump, Blueberry Mountain. The cars on the interstate make no sound. I can see the green life coming down from the granite passes, birches growing in frost heaves. The cars slow and never come again.

I try to think in geological time, when a mountain moves and a human century lives like the final stage of a dragonfly, a day to mate, a day to die. I let the tea cool in my tin cup, looking out into the layers of dark trees. Far out, a coyote howls. By firelight I stand before the picture of the last woman, the darkest figure, a stain upon the print. The paper picks up in the wind. The pine I have pinned it to is young and red, growing straight up toward sunlight. I sip my tea. It tastes like shale and hard water.

Josephine Earp moved north in the last big gold stampede. It was a later-comers' gold rush. A poor man's gold rush. It was easy to reach, not like Klondike farther inland. The streets were filled with yelling. A detachment of American soldiers kept order.

She is a black ghost. The dark hood becoming dark hair. Face upturned. There's high-class California family in that disdain, in the slightly curled lip, heavy, bored eyes.

Wyatt Earp, the gunslinger, murderer, wanted and found her, fell in love with the anger in the lift of her chin. They moved north, away from police records and stained reputations. He was down on his luck. Up north he and a friend built a club. Josie selected the thick carpets, fine mirrors, carved sideboards, the draperies, the paintings. She said The Dexter was better than anyplace in San Francisco. The border of the Arctic Circle, Bering Sea coast, Norton Sound. At the tip of a country.

She was still a beauty at thirty-seven. The woman in the black sheer shawl. With a scowl and heavy eyes. A knockout. She gambled wildly until Wyatt cut her off and asked all the other gambling houses to do the same. She stormed off on her own, lived off men who would indulge her. I wonder if she always got what she wanted. Josie, in black, somehow sad, fading at the edges. She could seep out and away.

Before the gambling she lost a child at birth. The only one she'd ever want, Wyatt's little boy. He was aging fast, too; his waxed mustache was all white and he wasn't quick on the draw. Ashamed, he never wore his pistols at The Dexter. While she was with rich men, maybe down in Dawson, he got in two bar fights. She came back to him. Statuesque, heavy breasts, hands deep in her lap. Shadows fill in everything else. She is so solid it is hard to imagine that she once danced. The skin of her neck must have smelled like winter's incense, cinnamon, a bit of charcoal, crushed roses, a dark, thick scent.

The gold was gone and the criminals and thieves and whores remained. It was a dirty city, so dirty the National Guard pulled back and left it to eat itself up. The buildings were black with rot. Tents were heavy with the constant rain. With her fortune and her husband, Josie left Alaska. Moved out silently, dragging her dark veil behind her. Two years later the high tsunami seas of the Bering would come in over the harbor, over the waterfront slums, to clean up the town.

The wave dragged the red-light district out into the ocean. Everything else was flooded, wrecked. Josie didn't see Dawson like that. I think she would have liked to, the damp wood beams and scattered clapboard, the bay filled with debris. There is something in the casual slump of her shoulders and the cruel lift of her head that wants it all to go away.

I have been staring at these pictures so long that sometimes I see the women smile or blink. I walk out into the woods and take down Morning's photo, white against the dark trunk. By the campsite I carefully fold the others and put them in my pack. I sit by the fire. There are no eyes on me. Sparks burst off. Up in the canopy they fade and stars shine, hazy summer sky. My fingers smell of wood smoke. It will not wash off for many days. It stays deep in the roots of hair, under fingernails, in the pores of my cheeks.

The stream laps against bedrock and I know I could pack up and move north, up through the mountains to the Canadian prairies, circle west along Hudson Bay, keep moving, find a hollow between kettle lakes where a man has not sat for hundreds of years. It is getting cold. My flesh stands up as if something were moving behind me. I do not turn around to check. It is wiser not to; I have learned this lesson before. Ghosts want very little to do with the living. They see a landscape as it once was — this little valley a bare pasture, the oak to the right the only shade tree.

I fall asleep on a slab of bedrock still warm from the sun. As the stars wheel in the patch of open sky, my body fades away. Its outline remains like chalk on the rock. By morning, that too has worn off. I stand knee-deep in the river. I bend and bring water to my face. The sun rises low through the trees, striking the opposite bank all gold. A heron rests on my shoulder, his long tail feathers brushing my back. The books are open but I cannot read a word. All the words are strange. I wake. It is time to go.

— Megan Baxter

August

We didn't like the idea of sinking
needles through our skin and besides,
being blood sisters was too clichéd,
so we pushed past the creaky pantry door
and sloshed a little red wine into
paper cups and had a toast, kneeling
on the kitchen floor with
little grains of sand
digging into our bare knees.
We'd wrapped old Halloween costume cloaks
around our shoulders
to add to the solemnity of the night.
The wine had poured too quickly,
so we each had maybe a quarter of a cup
and no intention of drinking it all.
We sipped, tilting our heads back
ever so slowly, until
just a few drops of wine got past our lips.
We forced ourselves to swallow,
and gulped water from the tap
to clear our mouths.
Water dripping down our faces,
we went outside,
watched moths slam their
tiny bodies against the screen door,
and poured the remaining wine

into the daylilies
as a sort of offering to the world.
The moon was nearly full,
and we clasped hands and
turned our faces to the midnight sky
before slipping inside again,
and lying our hot, sticky bodies
on cotton sheets,
listening to our own breath,
and the frantic song
of a thousand chirping crickets.

— Rosemary Bateman

Elephant

He got his elephant at a flea market in India;
it had been forgotten there by a traveling circus.
He supposed it was the elephant trainer's guidance
that gave it the look of satisfaction
by teaching it how to smile. Its lips stretched
back, constantly showing large teeth,
white like baby pigs.
Even as it slept, legs tucked under its body,
belly against the ground, the elephant grinned.
It didn't stop until he noticed small holes
made through the elephant's lip.
Thick, clear strings were looped through,
pulled back, and tied around
both of the elephant's ears.
He cut the strings and let its top lip
fall back and rest against the bottom one
where it stayed.

— Juliana Morgado

Proximities

My boyfriend told me to eat mud.

He wanted me to scoop up wet handfuls and smear it across my lips,
paint my face with it and rejoice in its redness.

He wanted me to slip into it and bury myself up past my chin,
so that the mineral aroma would flare into my nostrils.

He wanted me to gulp down mountains
that taste salty like life, and plateaus that
taste overripe, like death and cantaloupes
close to bursting.

When it was over, I asked him to kiss me.

He said no . . .
considering where your mouth has been.

— Maggie Johnston

Crybaby Moon

The baby on his knee talks. Uncle smiles as Evan gurgles words to him and my mother asks him not to leave. "Stay, Sam," Momma pleads slowly. She is like molasses on April mornings, already sticky with heat. I imagine pulling Momma down, stretching her, until the molasses reaches that fine line just before it breaks. She is begging.

"Another baby boy, Sylvia," Uncle says to make conversation. He pauses, hands clasped around his kneecaps to stand. "I need to go." Uncle grows upward until he is over six feet tall and hands the baby to Momma solemnly. He turns to me, the only girl out of four boys so far. "So you hear the road calling my name?" I am nine now, and I know this question, the signal he wants me to give. I cup my hand around my ear for the *yes* he wants. In the distance I hear it, and I nod, and he ruffles my hair as a thank-you.

"His first words . . ." Momma's voice carries softly toward Uncle's back until it meets the porch screening and the sound stops.

One leg into the car, Uncle says good-bye without guilt. He backs up quickly with the stick shift he says he'll teach me to drive next time he comes, honks, and accelerates. The brothers try to chase after him and trip in the dust clouds of his car; their ankles and shins bleed on untied shoelaces, but their heads are held up without tears. Momma sighs heavily, defeated, and I know I will be cleaning them up in the creek today, because it's my fault he left, because it's my fault I let Uncle escape.

The brothers hate being washed, so they whine to Momma, hate the smudge of water on their brown skin. As I scrub them, they tease me about the half days I spend in the creek letting the water roll over my shoulders. They don't understand how I can like the feel of slimy rocks against the backs of my legs, the cold gasp of my feet when they touch the icy water. But more than anything, I stay there to avoid the murky house. It's like I'm blind in there, in that house — it's too hard for me to see through the hot, chaotic rooms. I don't even try anymore. The brothers just can't see how I can like the icy tranquillity of the creek, the clear view below the surface when I open my eyes.

Momma waits with skillet in hand when I return three dripping boys. She's on the porch still, rocking to an old song she sings as a lullaby to the baby, but I don't see the baby, and she's looking toward the road instead of behind at the house, where I can imagine Evan crying and no one listening to pick him up. He's only ten months old, and I know I'll hear that lullaby for a thousand more months, in the middle of the night and between thunderclaps and when we're sick but not vomiting. There are ashes in Momma's skillet, not from breakfast, and I think there is no breakfast.

She pulls a lonely cigarette out of her dress pocket, lights it, and says to the porch screen, like it's one of the brothers who've asked about Daddy, "Your father is taking a long time helping with the railroad. I don't think they're going to pay him.

"He saw he had another son and then left again to work. He said the railroad called him, I guess the way the road calls Sam's name." Momma inhales too deeply after she says that, and sputters like she can't get her breath. She taps the cigarette against the iron edge of the pot and, careful now, watches the gray ash burn it up. The brothers look at me, unsure with feet shuffling, wet footprints dancing on the porch floor beside me. She's started taking small puffs again, inhaling lightly. Sometimes this is how I see her through her bedroom door crack, staring at my father's picture, fingers curling like smoke around the wood frame.

"Momma?" I ask.

"Damn," she says swiftly as the burning cigarette reaches her fingers. I shove the brothers inside the door and her eyes don't even move away from the road as the brothers stumble past her. I can see the bulge of the pale-striped pack through her dress. "I haven't done this in a while," she says.

Inside, the air is moist with sweat and the machinery of toy cars. Momma has let our living room become a nest for them, the brothers' ruined traffic jams resembling railroad tracks across the floor. The brothers are playing naked and wet, pushing the metal cars over their shoulders and heads, calling them hills and mountains. When I ask them, they say that wearing clothes slows down the car wheels and causes complete standstills on seams. Evan cries beyond the vrooming cars, and I am the only one walking toward him, so I push the record of Billie Holiday onto the phonograph machine, hoping that the rusty sound of her voice will convince the brothers to put on clothes and Momma to come take care of Evan crying to her. Momma hums along outside, her voice rising and coiling with Billie's at the ceiling. Evan quiets at the duet. We all wait for the low notes to come that Momma can't hit, the frustrated slap of the screen door as she comes inside to shut off the machine and cry with her eyes slitted between fingers.

*   *   *

By dinnertime, Momma is hoarse from trying to reach the notes of the song that always disappoints her, and her cigarettes are gone. The brothers whine that they are hungry again, that peanut butter can't fill up men even as they reach for my sandwiches, and Momma slaps at their sticky mouth-corners where the peanut butter burrows until their cheeks are covered in the smell. I know she is tired — I know it from the halfhearted way she slaps at them, letting the impact slice the air before it meets their skin. "If you want dinner, make it yourself."

I unscrew the peanut butter lid again and turn the knife back into it, over and over, spreading the peanut butter thick onto bread the way I like it. Momma's face is turned away toward the window, thumb tucked under her chin, and her rough fingers take my sandwich from the plate.

The brothers look up, expecting a sandwich for each of them now, expecting me to do it because they think they're holy. The three are named 'the Gospels' by the girls at the school who don't know enough New Testament to realize they're missing a John. Daddy's name is John, but Momma refused to name Evan after him, because it was like naming a baby for months spent away at a time.

"No, you're going to have to make them yourself," I say. They whine to the chorus of the Billie Holiday song, and I can see Momma's eyes sharpen into focus and her jaw grow more pointed with each chew.

"No," I tell the brothers again, and tie the bread closed.

"Momma . . ."

She turns to face me so fast her dress swirls between her legs.

"Why do my children have to be so damn annoying? Jesus, just make them sandwiches, Kate." She folds back into her chair, crumpling slowly. The brothers give smooth glances back at me, at the peanut butter still open, still holy and untouched. They shrug off Momma's words from their shoulders, and they all float toward me, words and brothers, until I feel like I can't escape any of them. *Do you hear the road calling my name?*

The tears that come are heavy, and I try to brush off Momma's words like the brothers did to stop my tears, push the words off me, but I can't move them and water is sliding down my cheek and I know crying is even more annoying, but I can't stop. "Momma, I . . ."

She walks into her bedroom, slamming the door, and in my mind I can see her fingers reaching to outline Daddy's picture, just running her hardened fingertips over the wood that's smooth by now. Matthew slaps bread and peanut butter into sandwiches for all of them and says, "You're a crybaby, Kate. You cry at everything."

"Yeah," say the others, brown sticky mouths barely pulled apart by the word. "Crybaby."

Tears keep running down my cheeks until I hear Momma's slow ascent up the stairs toward me, and I make myself stop, I make myself wipe my eyes one last time. Her footsteps throb the wood in time with my hands smoothing the tear streaks on my face. Momma's breathing is heavy with apology when she knocks the door open with her foot. She says, "Thank —" and "Sorry about —" in a low voice before she cuts herself off in the middle of the awkward sounds. She leans against the door frame and closes her eyes. Finally she says, "Kate, this just isn't a good time to ask for Easter dresses, do you understand?"

I understand more than she does, that we can just afford peanut butter sandwiches every day, that Daddy's paychecks don't come thick enough when we need them, but in the sunlight floating in the window, her eyes look golden and unearthly and I'm thinking this might not be my mother, it might not be. I stifle my thought and say yes.

"Sam left this morning because you said yes to him. He left because of you," she says loudly. "You are not going to cry to him for help, do you understand? You won't tell him about wearing last year's dress for Easter Sunday." Her voice is fierce and mean.

"Yes, Momma," I say quietly to my hands. When Momma is like this, like molasses, I don't want to break her so I nod along with what she says, even though I have never told Uncle that I won't get what I want; he just knows somehow because he says we're alike, and gives it to me in surprises. Momma says more softly that she is making taffy downstairs and when it is ready to pull I need to watch the brothers so Evan won't get any. "Yes, Momma." The murky air of the house, cigarette presence and tears and hot lonely despair, fills up in front of my eyes even when I say my escape words to get out of the house.

"Where are you going? To the creek again?"

"Yes, Momma."

Uncle calls three days before Easter when the clouds stick to the treetops like Momma's taffy did. "Hello from the Easter Bunny," he says.

"Hello?" I say to him.

72

"I'm calling because a little birdie told me you had something you wanted to tell me."

I imagine a seagull flying between the house and the North Carolina shore where Uncle lives, listening to the conversation Momma had with me. I think of the Easter dress I would like, pink with white lace and a lavender hat, and I wonder if maybe Uncle will rescue me in the car that causes dust clouds so big the brothers trip on them, take me to a department store to pick it out. I tell him quickly that I want an Easter dress. I tell him the color doesn't even matter, that I don't even like pink or lace all that much anyway.

"Thank you," he says, and I can see him ruffling my hair over the telephone line. *Do you hear the road calling my name?*

"But I'm a crybaby," I say slowly, like I just remembered. I don't want to tell him, but I'm wondering if that's what the seagull meant, what the seagull told him I wanted to say.

To change the subject, I ask him if there is any news at the beach, a place I've never been, and he says, "Down by the sea there is no news. The waves just swallow it up." He asks to speak to Momma.

Momma climbs the porch stairs as he talks, Evan asleep in her arms, and after she puts him down I hold out the telephone to her. "It's Uncle Sam — he wants to talk to you," I say, and she takes the phone carefully, like she holds Evan.

"Sam, what is it?" She is quiet, hands bent behind her hips, and straightens a stray strand of hair that has curled from the sun. "We're fine. We're *fine*, Sam. You trust a nine-year-old for the truth?"

She turns around toward me but I am gone, pressed against

the back door, ready to run all the way to North Carolina and the ocean.

"She bends things because . . . because she wants a dress, Sam! Is that what you wanted to hear? That I can't even provide my daughter a new Easter dress?"

I trace the door frame until I hear her voice calm down, brushing my fingers over the wood's knobby holes, trying to find comfort like Momma does, but it doesn't work like it should.

Momma sighs when she puts the receiver back into its cradle, and I hear her ask herself, "Why wasn't that the man I married?"

Below the surface of the creek I hope Momma's words will make sense, because it's like they're boxed inside my head; they repeat but I still don't understand their sentences, even with my eyes open under the water. *Why wasn't that the man I married? Why wasn't that the man I married?* In my mind I try to switch the brothers around from the way I know it happened — Daddy now the best man, and Uncle standing next to Momma's white-dressed body at the altar when she says she marries him. But I can't do it, and instead I imagine just myself, not them, at their wedding, wearing a lacy pink dress with a lavender hat, and that's all I see in the water until I close my eyes.

On Easter morning I wake up with a basket full of sea-green fabric inside my door, ruffled sleeves hidden among the cloth, a lace collar. The tag says, *A gift from the coast — the Easter Bunny*, and I think of the seagull that flies between North Carolina and the house, the way it must have carried the basket in its beak for miles like the stork. Momma hides a smile into her water when I show her the basket, and I can see it reflected a hundred times in the different angles of glass, so it's like she's smiling a hundred times, like she's showing me all the smiles I've deserved at once.

At church, brothers in blue suits tight on their elbows, it's crowded with hats and bustles of skirts complimenting me. I smile as Momma shuffles me from woman to woman before the organist begins pressing keys, just smiling as I walk in pinching shoes and keep running the sea-green cloth through my fingers. I wait quietly for my favorite part of the service, only moving the creases of my dress during the hymns, and finally it comes — the Registration of Attendance, the paper announcement where families sign their names to prove they came. Momma sometimes lets me write her name and all the brothers' for printing practice, even though it's Sunday and it's against the Ten Commandments to work. *Sylvia Hegill*, I print under the cream Member side, and underneath I list *Matthew Hegill, Mark Hegill, Luke Hegill, Evan Hegill, and Mrs. Sam Hegill.*

I'm sitting on the end of the pew, and as I'm pressing the pencil to paper, I come to the decision that if Momma couldn't marry Uncle, maybe I could because I'm a step later in being related. Momma doesn't see me sign myself as Uncle's wife, but she can see me in the sea-green dress from the coast and that's enough, I think.

The next time Uncle comes, the time he promised to teach me to drive, he greets me with "Down by the sea there is no news. The waves swallow it up" before I can even ask, like it's another signal or catchword between us.

"I have news," Matthew says. "Kate's a crybaby. Nothing's swallowed that up."

"I'm sure she's not," Uncle says, "because I'm about to teach her to drive."

"Sam," Momma says, "she's nine and it's nighttime." She holds Evan hesitantly; she's not sure whether the man Evan said his first words to will want to fold his arms to hold the baby. The brothers whine like crickets.

"There's a full moon," Uncle says. "The field will be slow with mud. She's responsible." He swings the door open for me and tells me to start the motor. The keys tremble in the ignition when I touch them, foot against the clutch; I grin and Momma walks back over the porch stairs, pacing, until she sees Uncle lean his body into the driver's seat. We drive without talking to a crop-rotating field where the sun beams nutrients back into the soil, next year's corn crop. "Can you see? The moon gives everything a white coating," he says when our bodies arrive with the car. I nod.

"So life has been treating you as a crybaby?"

"The brothers have."

"Did you know . . . did you know the man in the moon," Uncle says in a deep, drawn-out voice, "is a crybaby?"

I turn my eyes to the moon, full in the sky, trying to search out the silvery teardrops Uncle says drip from his eyes, but I only see melting shades of gray, and I keep trying to see what I want to believe is there.

"Do you not see the dark spots, the craters?" Uncle says, pointing. "The man in the moon has cried so many tears, craters have spread onto his face, miles deep and wide."

I smile, and he asks me if I am ready to drive, if I am ready to hear the road calling my name. "Thank you," I say, ruffling my hands over the wheel, and I start the ignition, foot just touching the clutch, driving slowly toward my creek that eventually reaches the ocean.

— Sarah Campbell

Numbers

My husband, Tim, hated it when I started spewing numbers. We'd sit at the breakfast table, him drinking coffee and reading the *Wall Street Journal*, me drinking black tea and doing the crossword puzzle in *People*, only because I wanted something to do with my hands, and I'd say, "Did you know that I'm the same size as Vivien Leigh in *Gone With the Wind*?"

"Really, Amy." His voice wouldn't even rise in pitch.

"She was five foot three and a half. Twenty-three-inch waist, thirty-three hips." I'd take a sip of my tea and set down the mug on the edge of my magazine. "We're the exact same proportions," I'd say. Tim would nod his head, and his arms would bob up and down, holding the paper.

I didn't even like math as a kid. When the class would go up to the board in third grade to solve multiplication problems, I'd break into a sweat. My mother hauled me to various doctors and made me start wearing deodorant when I was seven. Now all I seemed to do was memorize numbers: the year of George Reeves's suicide, my likelihood of getting pregnant after I reached my forties, weather forecasts for all the major world capitals. I didn't learn stocks or bonds or any of that. They didn't make sense to me. I liked what I referred to as social numbers, ones you could use in conversation. They were the kind printed in *Cosmopolitan* or *Entertainment Weekly*, or even that special section they do in *Time* every issue, with the statistics of dead soldiers and the nation's spending on fast food. Or *Harper's*, with its index of every imaginable number for the month.

"Did you know that McDonald's bought something like one-fifth of last year's potato crop?" I said when Tim and I were watching television. He stared at the screen and didn't say anything. We sat for a few minutes in silence until I looked over at him and asked, "Well, what do you think?"

"What? Oh." He shrugged his shoulders. "Well, Amy, it's not really surprising. It makes sense."

"Don't you think it's a little weird, one company having that kind of money and control?"

"I guess," he said. "It's not really any of my business. They can do whatever they want with their money. It's not like I can stop them." He drummed his fingers on the remote for a few seconds, then changed the channel.

The Gallup Poll did things for me that boyfriends and husbands could never even touch. New ones came out every day, and I'd sit in bed with my laptop, reading each one. I'd discovered the Gallup Poll in college. I was never the type to read a newspaper from cover to cover. Typically I just read the Living section, where I learned how to make birdbaths out of Popsicle sticks or read about the can-do seven-year-old with some crazy amount of community service. My roommate pointed out the results of a survey to me one day, though, and that's when I became obsessed. Gallup Polls were like high school dances to me: flirtation with the facts without the hassle of commitment. I didn't have to know the how or why, just statistics and pie charts and brightly colored bar graphs. People like me didn't ever want to know why, because knowing meant forming an attachment of some kind.

I first got obsessed with numbers in high school. My younger sister, Allison, who was twelve to my seventeen, decided to memorize pi one summer. She stopped at sixty-seven digits because she said learning all that information was giving her a headache. I thought she was being lazy. She had a habit of stopping things before she ever came close to accomplishing her goals. Still, every time my parents gave a dinner or went to my summer dance recitals, Allison got the attention.

"Say a few numbers," my mother asked her at a friend's birthday party. "Say some."

"Three, one, four, one, five . . ."

She continued, but I didn't listen. I didn't want to admit that maybe her talents could exceed mine, that maybe for once my younger sister could do something better than I could. I knew I was acting like a selfish brat, but I didn't care. If she got more attention, then I would just have to beat her at what she did best.

It started out with formulas. I hated math, but I could name every single equation in my trigonometry textbook. I didn't know how to use any of them, but just knowing them gave me some sense of relief. Instead of doing homework, I read the glossary, where they showed how to measure the sides of right triangles and had the diagrams of sine waves that looked like the stale ribbon candy my grandmother bought me every Christmas. It was only a matter of time before I was memorizing recipes and metric conversions. Most people didn't think my rote memorization was fascinating the way I did, so for a while I tried to stop, but with no luck. What I possessed bordered on a personality disorder, if not a chemical imbalance, but I forced myself to learn as many numbers as possible. I couldn't have stopped even if I'd wanted to.

Eventually I moved on to odd scientific findings. I found that people who wear socks while they sleep live an average of five minutes longer than people who don't, and drinking red wine can lower your blood pressure and cholesterol by something like thirty percent. *Social numbers*, I told myself. That's where it got fun. A lot of the time, though, I wasn't quite sure about the numbers. I would remember them incorrectly, or I would use what other people called "questionable sources." For some reason most of my friends didn't consider *In Style* a reliable place for information, even though I know they had to believe that eighty-eight percent of women use a blow-dryer to style their hair. You can't hear a number like that and just ignore it.

The polls were what got me. I couldn't get enough of them. *USA Today* often published the Gallup Poll, my personal favorite, in conjunction with CNN.

"Tim," I said one night in October when we were playing Scrabble, "eighty-eight percent of Americans approve of the way the president is doing his job."

He held the silver bag full of letters and shook some out into his hand. "So?" he said.

"That's what the Gallup Poll said," I told him.

"I'm going to get a beer. You want one?" I shook my head. Tim stood up, stretched his arms, and walked into the kitchen.

"You know Diane Lane only has a twenty-five-inch waist?" I called after him.

He walked back into the living room. "Where'd you find that?"

"*Celebrity Sleuth*. They listed all the measurements of the actresses they consider most beautiful. She was on there." I placed three letters on the board.

Tim looked over my shoulder. "Pox." He took a sip of his drink. "Does that even count? Don't you need to put 'chicken-pox' on there?"

"It's a word," I said. "A disease. It doesn't have to be specific like that. It can just be 'pox.'" I glanced up at him. "You know, twelve million people died from Spanish influenza in the epidemic."

Tim shrugged his shoulders and started walking to the bedroom. "Fifty percent of marriages end in divorce," he said. "But like it even matters anyway."

"Fifty-six percent of people think we should increase government spending," I said during breakfast the next day. "I don't understand why."

Tim looked at me over the edge of his newspaper. "Some people think that we need to focus more money on protecting ourselves. It's not a bad idea, really."

"The government spent thirteen hundred dollars on lapel pins last year for the White House staff," I said. "Or maybe it was thirteen thousand. Lapel pins. Jesus. I could have paid off my credit cards with that kind of money."

"I'm going out of town next week," said Tim. "You'll be okay for a few days, right?"

"Yeah, I'll be fine. Of course, my chances of getting raped will probably go up."

"What?"

"You know. People might not know you're out of town, but they'll just somehow know that I'm more vulnerable."

"Because they're psychic."

"*Yes.*"

Tim left for five days. I know he was probably trying to get away from me for a while. I knew my numbers must have gotten on his nerves, but I couldn't stop. The days he was gone, I spent all my time watching CNN and reading USA *Today* and the Gallup Poll and *Harper's*. I knew I was alienating Tim. I called in sick at work and stayed in the house the whole five days, worrying about where he was. He hadn't told me where he was going, and I didn't have any clue. I didn't sleep at all. Eighty-five percent of Americans approved of the war we fought against terrorists. Forty-four percent identified more with the Republican Party. Thirteen percent couldn't make up their minds, though, so I figured I'd be okay eventually.

Tim got back while I was out teaching at the community college. I did night classes there in writing. No one even questioned where I'd been for a week. They probably blamed it on my artistic temperament. I came home to find Tim sitting in front of the television, flipping channels. "How was your trip?" I asked.

"Fine."

I sat down beside him. "You know Frank Capra was only five foot seven. I found that out today."

"What?"

"You know," I said. "Frank Capra. *It's a Wonderful Life.* All those propaganda movies for the government. That kind of thing."

"Oh, yeah."

Maybe it had always been like this with us and I'd never noticed it before. I knew he wasn't listening, but I didn't really care. I kept memorizing numbers and telling myself that if I could learn just one more fact, everything would be fine. With numbers, the more I knew, the easier a time I had trying to figure things out. You gained reason from numbers — or at least that's what I kept telling myself.

Sometimes Tim and I didn't talk at all. On those nights we watched television or sat at the kitchen table and read newspapers. We were up late one night, and I looked over my paper at him. "Seventy-one percent of Americans agree with the way the president has handled the economy," I said in a tired voice, trying to initiate some kind of conversation so we wouldn't be sitting in silence.

Tim looked at me. "Amy." His voice was flat.

"What?"

"I don't care, okay? I don't care." He walked to the sink, got a cup, and poured himself some water. It was as though he couldn't even stand to look me in the eye.

"About what?" I put down my paper and drummed my fingers on the tabletop.

"All those numbers." Tim gulped down his water and wiped his mouth with the back of his hand. "Those statistics and measurements and those random things you always talk about. I don't care. I don't want to hear about them anymore."

I glared at him. "Well, I don't want to hear what you care about, either," I said. "I don't want to know what you're doing or what you've done or what really makes you happy right that moment."

Tim said, "Amy, it doesn't matter. It's not a big deal. Don't get so worked up about it."

I could barely breathe. "Why is it not a big deal? You're making it sound like a big deal. You knew I'd think it was a big deal."

"It's really not."

"Thirty-three percent more Colombians have gone missing or been killed in the past year."

"Yes. And?"

"I just wanted to remind you. In case you forgot."

Tim walked into the living room. "Why did you think I'd even know that in the first place?" he asked. He turned back to look at me.

I shrugged my shoulders. "I don't know. Knowing you, I thought you might."

I didn't know if I was pushing Tim away from me or if he was purposely avoiding me. It got to the point where I couldn't tell anymore. I had to wonder about the out-of-town trip. He never said anything about it to me, except when he first got back and I'd asked. Pretty soon he was taking more and more trips away from me, never even bothering to see if I wanted to go, the way he had in the past. There had to be another woman, another person, or maybe he was just trying to get away from me and the endless Gallup Polls I'd started clipping from the newspaper and tacking up on the kitchen bulletin board. Whatever it was, Tim did his best to hide it from me.

I still had my obsession with what I called social numbers, but I eventually got caught up in other ones, too. Stocks, which I'd always claimed to hate before, were now a great interest of mine.

There were so many of them, and of course they always changed. The stock market was like a *Harper's* index increased exponentially and gone absolutely crazy. There were so many more numbers.

Tim got home from work one evening, and as soon as he walked in the door, I said, "The Dow Jones Industrial Average was down one-point-two points today." He turned around and walked back outside. I heard his car start, and the wheels spun on the gravel driveway.

He didn't come back for a week after that. We stopped talking completely, except for the necessary phrases. I began memorizing historical dates and Internet addresses. Tim spent more time away from me, and I didn't blame him.

One night, Tim didn't come home at all. He called me late in the evening and said, "I'm staying somewhere else tonight. Don't worry about me."

"Well, where are you staying?" I asked. "Can I have your number there in case something happens?"

"I'll be home in the morning; don't worry about it." He hung up in my ear.

I sighed. Maybe it was my choice of words that did it. I shouldn't have said anything about numbers.

There was a Charles Schwab office downtown that had a ticker for the New York Stock Exchange outside the door. I noticed it one night on my way back from work, and now I passed by it every time I could. The way the numbers never stopped fascinated me. They never stayed the same long enough for me to care about them.

One night, I stood across the street from the office. Tim had stopped calling regularly almost a month before. I'd brought a thermos with me, to warm my hands, and now I leaned against the back of my car, staring at the ticker. It was cold, and I wanted to go home, but I couldn't move. I just watched the numbers pass me by, never pausing, always in a hurry to be somewhere besides here.

I felt a tap on my shoulder, and I jumped.

"Hey." It was Tim.

"Don't do that again," I said. "You scared me."

He looked at the ticker, then back at me. "I figured I'd find you here," he said. "I tried calling you, but no one picked up."

I glared at him. "What am I supposed to do, sit around and wait for you? I've been waiting for weeks."

"So have I." He blew his breath out, leaned against the car, and stared at the Charles Schwab sign. "When are you going to stop with all those numbers? I can't take being at that house with you if that's all you're going to do."

"Fifty percent of marriages. Fifty percent."

"Yes, you've told me that before."

I stared straight in front of me. "You still haven't gotten the hint."

"Was that one?"

"I don't know. You decide." I walked around the car and got in the driver's side. "I'm going back to the house now. Do you want to come with me?"

Tim stood up straight and stretched his arms. "Probably not."

"Will I see you when I get back then?"

"I don't know."

He walked away, probably back to his car, but I couldn't be sure. I started the car and pulled out of the parking space, into the street. I rolled down my window and stared at the sidewalk when I stopped at a traffic light. I started whispering to myself, "Three, one, four, one, five," over and over again, the only digits I could remember and the only ones that even mattered to me anymore.

— Charlotte Seaman–Huynh

Something in the Air

Dramatis Personae

Luster is your eccentric physics teacher who used to be a bounty hunter. He produces a feeling inconceivable to anyone who has never experienced him, like smoking pot. "To those who haven't, an explanation is impossible. To those who have, none is needed."

I remember the days when **Panos** and I would raise the flag together in fifth grade, discussing the *Today Show* and making cracks about Bob Dole, the air young and crisp. I remember our awkward, pubescent middle school years when afternoon fun was tearing around the neighborhood on bikes and kicking over trash cans.

Mitchell is always half drunk with some scheme in his pocket. Some weeklong fascination or goddamn quirk. And it is right for him, just his constitution.

Jux is my friend who I want to be. He knows more than you do about Woody Guthrie.

Kenneth Paul is a fifty-year-old Anglican reverend who speaks with an upper-class Louisiana accent. Sort of a drawl hyphen between Justin Wilson and Tony Blair. He always carries a bottle of Tabasco with him.

Tom is the street musician you really enjoyed two days ago but didn't give any money to.

Lars is breakfast and a cigarette at one in the afternoon.

Otto is the ideal American boy, your childhood friend. You guys traded baseball cards and stuffed firecrackers in apples when you were kids.

Mr. Milton cares, though it's hard to these days.

I.

In physics with my head spinning, knowing the less I pay attention now the more work it will be later. That realization has no effect on me, however, and I decide to play with the tuning forks in the back. I understand it will be another late Thursday copying notes and bullshitting worksheets, but it's OK because we've made a C chord with the tuning forks. Luster pauses his notes and gives us a knowing nod. Panos has realized that although Luster seems dense and foolish, he's actually one of the smartest people we know. We are all far below him and he has decided it's a waste of time and energy to lower himself to our level.

II.

I can't sleep so I listen to My Morning Jacket and pore over stacks of my pictures, my proof of having been. I find one of Panos and me in Michigan that summer, my uncle's cottage on the lake. We're standing next to each other on the beach, squinting at the morning sun, the lake in the background. I never seem to remember that during the summer Lake Michigan water is always cold as hell. We always made a point to swim, though, inching our way out, tense, flinching whenever a wave came in.

"We'll get used to it eventually," we'd tell each other, but of course we never did. Panos is stubborn like that, though. I was surprised that he connected so well with my family, soft-spoken loner that he is.

We chilled on the boardwalk in the middle of the night, smoking cigarettes and looking for shooting stars, listening to the rolling waves below, trying to deconstruct life, what we knew of it anyway.

III.

It's a Lars and Isaac spring break. We're either shoveling in Mongolian barbecue or avoiding Neal, sitting in Broad Ripple or drinking in the basement. Being bored isn't quite so bad with two people.

Tonight we're waiting for Otto to stop hanging out with Macy, eating Skittles in Broad Ripple and averting our eyes from the Bridge Kids, listening to the Ramones and enjoying the breeze. End up in my room watching that skate video I never gave back to Cali and that Modest Mouse bootleg I got offa eBay.

Although we've spent the past five days together we haven't said shit to each other — funny like that. I keep expecting and hoping we'll have some intense conversations and come to some earth-shattering realizations — like him and Ooghs realizing it was Ooghs who hit Anders's stepbrother's girlfriend's car two years ago — but we don't.

My attempts at deep conversation lead Lars to tell me how Goths used to hang out at amusement parks. "I always went to amusement parks when I was a kid. I didn't really like the rides but the Goths were interesting." I ask him why they hung out at amusement parks. "I dunno, gotta hang out somewhere I guess."

He makes me remember that Sarah Vowell story in which she gets a Goth makeover for a night in San Francisco. Apparently it takes some two hours to get "gothed out," and there's a rule that a Goth has to spend at least as much time in costume at the club as it takes to get ready. It's all about being seen.

I'm reading it out loud to Lars and he falls asleep on my futon. But who needs deep conversation when you've got a Modest Mouse bootleg?

IV.

Gilbert rambling on on on about tone and diction and me thinking what would I get tattooed on myself. I think you can tell a lot about a person by what they decide to have burned into their skin with colored ink. It's like deciding what shirt to wear, but to the umpteenth.

When Jux turned 18 he went to town as far as tattoos are concerned. Matching tribal symbols on his shoulders. Another on his chest. A dragonfly on his arm. Very raw, very Jux.

Lars was excited about the idea, too, when he turned 18 but waited and chose carefully, getting the word **SOUL** stamped on his chest. Lars may be a scrawny white kid but he's got more Soul than a lot of people I know.

When I was visiting Beloit I kept hearing these two guys referring to their friend who'd "just found out where the sidewalk ends." I kept wondering what the hell they were talking about. Apparently there's a girl on campus who has the drawing from the cover of Shel Silverstein's *Where the Sidewalk Ends* tattooed below her belly button, leading right down. Wonderfully poetic.

V.

It seems like everyone always wants what they don't have. Teenagers want to drink and have sex and be old, adults want to be young again. The slacker wishes he was smart, the smart kid wishes he was a slacker. The homeless guy wants stability, the stable guy wants adventure. On and on.

I suppose Buddhist monks are sitting at the crossroads on this one. *All life is suffering, suffering stems from desire. Curb desire, curb suffering.* There's beauty in tranquillity like that, but I don't think I'm cut out for it.

Back when no one could drive it was always, "It's gonna be so awesome when I can drive. We'll be able to go Anywhere, Anytime!" Now that everyone can drive we're satiated and it's always, "Remember when we used to walk everywhere, hang out all the time?" with a reminiscent stare on our faces. "That was so much fun. Order Jack's and watch *Stand by Me* at Otto's."

VI.

At some Brebeuf party I run across Amy, whom Panos and Otto took Driver's Ed with. I tell her my name and she gets that look in her eyes and I can feel the oncoming "Are you Mitchell's brother?!" all wide-eyed, a mix of awe and disgust. She tells us how he unsuccessfully tried to get with her sister in the darkroom two years ago and we laugh because it seems so right. The darkroom. You'd always hear some story about Mitchell. Panos thinks for a moment and says, "Of all the stories we *have* heard about Mitchell, think about how many there are we just haven't heard."

VII.

Tom is wise in that way that people who've lived in the same city for fifty years are. Him and Mr. Payne. He can pull off the button-down shirt with the American flag on it, his white beard and sunglasses.

He tells me how there used to be a swamp south of Kessler by Carvel, until a couple of brothers drowned and they filled it in with sand. He graduated from Broad Ripple in 1961, one year after Letterman, though he prefers Leno now. "That Letterman's always been a smart-ass," he tells me, sipping his coffee.

"Can't stand cops," he says, frowning. He's been playing guitar on the street for twenty years and still gets hassled for panhandling, though he's never asked anyone for money.

He likes to sing old rock 'n' roll and has a deep, beautiful, bellowing voice. I lean awkwardly against the wall, sorry I don't have anything besides a quarter and my dollar for the Metro.

Girls smile as they walk by him, drunk guys yell and give him money. "I LOVE THIS GUY!!" I toss my quarter in his case, tell him it's everything but my bus money. "Gotta have bus money!" he tells me with a grande smile.

VIII.

"Feel it," he would tell me, "those notes on the paper don't matter. Just feel it." And I'd play. And I did feel it, but knew I didn't have the technical discipline I could if I wasn't so damn lazy. "You can break the rules all ya want, you just gotta learn 'em first." I was his last hope, his work in progress. And I knew I let Mr. Milton down.

He'd show me pictures of his old students, playing with Freddie Hubbard and Wynton Marsalis and Dave Brubeck. It always gave me that feeling in my stomach, watching a sweet breeze of memories wash over him. "Now this here's Stanley Moore, graduated" — he'd look up at the ceiling for a moment — "woulda been in eighty-three. Came in as a freshman, hadn't played a note in his life. Daddy'd left him, Momma was all sortsa messed up. I started him on tenor, he'd stay after till six or seven o'clock every day. I'd tell him, 'Stanley, you gotta go home sometime, man, I can't stay here all night.' 'Jus lemme run through this one more time,' he'd tell me." Mr. Milton would laugh real hard with a big smile on his face. "Time he was a junior he was a good player. Now he's playin' with Lee Morgan at the Vanguard in New York." Mr. Milton loved that, talking about his old students.

He was an institution, though these days it seemed like he was one of the few left. The system was failing him. No one wanted to support music when half the kids couldn't read or write. No one cared anymore, and you could see it in his face, in his hands that shook just slightly, deep creased, well worn, resting easily on the back of a chair. Mr. Milton was fighting a losing battle, and he knew it. So he looked to me, 'cause he knew I had it in me, knew I could be a Stanley Moore if I tried, if I wanted to. If I'd just *feel* it.

IX.

Outside the church lots of kids hang out, talking, smoking, being loud. The pizza's not here yet so I sit down on the ground and tug at my shirtsleeves. A couple of punks hang around on the porch, screaming from time to time. None of these kids fit in elsewhere but here they seem to meld and coexist beautifully, creating an equilibrium of persons. The sexy redhead cancels out the homely blond, the Korn guy cancels out the Emo guy, the punks cancel me out.

A guy in a vest walks up to Panos with a feather in his hand. "Close your eyes and tell me what this feels like." Panos leans away instinctively as Vest tries to brush his face with the feather.

"C'mon, man" — Panos's epitaph.

"I'm not gonna do anything, just close your eyes and tell me what this feels like."

Vest eventually gives up on Panos and moves over to me. "Close your eyes and tell me what this feels like." I shut them, flinching slightly, not sure what to expect. I feel the feather on my face.

"Just feels like a feather, man." He moves on, managing a different response from each person he tests.

I breathe in slowly, tasting the smell of cheap cigarettes and denim jackets. Tugging at my sleeves again, I glance around, looking at everyone, studying everyone. What is it that brings us here every Saturday? Is it really the free pizza or is it because we're looking for someplace to belong, just like everyone else? None of us think about it that way, but I think that's why. We're too proud of not being accepted by everyone else to take comfort in the acceptance Free Pizza Night offers.

On the steps, two guys stare intently at their chess game, deep in thought. Over in the parking lot the skaters try hard but never actually land a trick, which only seems to make them more determined.

— Tucker Eads

97

Lifethreads

Analya had been marked as a Weaver for as long as she could remember. Innumerable times in her life she had listened to her parents proudly recalling how, even as a baby, she had been fascinated by threads. As she had grown, the indications had continued to appear: uneasiness around scissors, unexplainable pickiness about the blanket on her bed, a tendency to twist her hair into tangles so complex that they couldn't be unraveled. Her parents had smiled and indulged her, knowing how honored they were to have a future Weaver in the family.

The other children, too, knew that Analya was special. They had heard from their parents how rare and special Weavers were — only three or four born every year in the entire country. As a result, even though Analya was an only child, she never lacked for playmates; she was always surrounded by a crowd of children jostling for a place in her favor. Despite this crowd, Analya had only a couple of true friends, two girls born only a week before her named Taliya and Parladi. Taliya was the Brunatis' second daughter and lived with her parents and sister several blocks away. Parladi was an only child who lived only with her mother; her father had disappeared soon after her birth. None of the children wondered about Parladi's father — every once in a while, people would disappear. That was simply the way of things.

For the first five years of her life, Analya basked in the popularity and comfort her status brought her. Then one day while she was out playing with the other children, Analya began fiddling with a loose thread on her dress. Idly twisting and toying

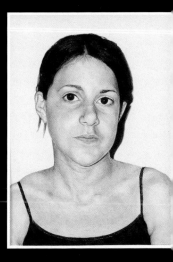

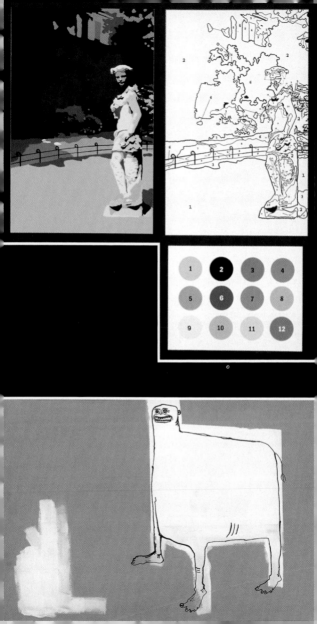

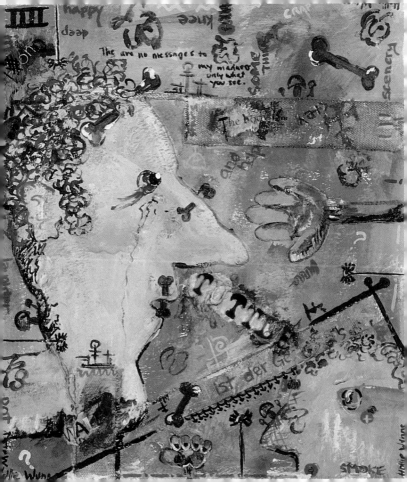

12

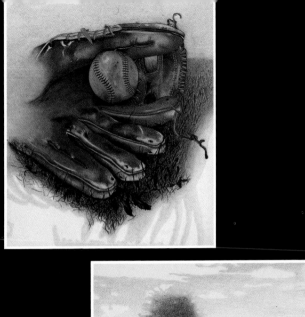

16

Art credits: page 1 top, Gelaina Poth, *Neptune Rising*; bottom, Gregory Larse
Love; page 2 top, David Noyce, *Looking at the Night Sky*; bottom, Jeremy Hyma
Self-Portrait; page 3 top, Dustin Neece, *The Bowler — Self-Portrait*; bottom, Micha
Enriquez, *Speed of Light*; page 4 top, Jonathan E. Dones, *Solitude*; bottom, Angely
Castelli, *Swimmer*; page 5 top left, Elechi Kadete, *Self-Portrait*; top right, Joan
Dur, *Jamie*; bottom, Tuka Lager, *9/11*; page 6 top, Matthew Doeringer, *Untitle*
bottom, Caleb Sears, *If I Only Had Arms*; page 7 top, Amanda Cates, *32nd Note
bottom, Armen Danilian, *Trophy*; page 8, Paul Thompson, *Adam and Eve*; pa
9 top left, Harold Julian, *Unwanted*; top right, Hector A. J. Ortiz, *Revealing Myse*
bottom, Molly Moss, *The Sixth Sense*; page 10, Katherine Pfeiffer, *Ben*; page 1
Hollie Wynne, *It's Only What You See*; page 12 top left, Ian Ferguson, *Trash*; top rig
Ian Ferguson, *Anika*; bottom, Sarah Saul, *Oblivion*; page 13, Parker Michels, *Seve*
page 14, Anne Joseph, *Sept. 11th, Brooklyn*; page 15 top, Ronald Rabideau, *Untitle*
bottom, Ana Rodriguez, *An Apple a Day*; page 16, James Millerton, *Soul Mate*

with it, she soon formed a knot. At that instant, a large branch on a nearby tree shuddered, cracked, and fell — landing only inches away from several of the children. From then on, Analya's crowd of admirers grew smaller each day, as the other children (and their parents) learned to fear what Analya might unknowingly do. Even Parladi soon stopped coming to play, tensely explaining that she just didn't feel safe around Analya. Only Taliya remained close to Analya, continuing to play with her despite what the other children whispered. On the day the branch fell, Analya felt for the first time the burden of having a Weaver's talents.

A week after the branch incident, three full Weavers visited Analya's family; somehow they knew what had occurred. They told her parents that Analya was coming into her abilities early and must begin her training for the safety of all those around her. One of the Weavers, a slim, kind-eyed woman who introduced herself as Malati, presented Analya with an intricately wrought charm in the shape of a loom that would identify Analya as a Weaver to all who saw her. Analya added the charm onto the necklace that she, like every other child and adult, wore, placing it between the colored beads that displayed her family's pattern. This necklace, which identified her family to anyone who saw her, would now also reveal her special talents and status.

From that day on, Analya began her education as a Novice Weaver. She continued to live at home, but every day she walked to the Weavers' Complex in the center of town. There, along with several other children, she learned about the Weavers' Arts: Taleweaving and Spellweaving. Malati, her primary teacher and mentor, told Analya that what had happened with the branch was an example of Spellweaving.

"Anyone," she explained, "can play with a string and make a knot. A Weaver's talent allows that string and that knot to become a spell that causes something — like the falling of a branch — to occur." Malati taught her students all the different forms of Spellweaving: knots, braids, and chains. As time passed, Analya learned the various ways Spellweaving could affect reality, ways that ranged from setting and healing a broken bone to calling a storm or starting a fire without wood.

At the same time, another teacher, named Naran, instructed the children in the art of Taleweaving. Naran was a kindly man but a strict teacher, always pushing his students to learn as much and as quickly as he felt they could. From him, Analya learned how to weave emotions and events, progressing from Weaving as someone else told a story to Weaving stories of her own creation into blankets. She learned to read the blankets created by other Weavers, seeing and feeling the stories in her mind as she ran her fingers over the lines of thread. Later, she was taught how to Weave blankets that didn't require a Weaver to interpret them, that could draw the minds of anyone who saw them into the Tale she wove.

During the four years Analya spent as a Novice, she learned swiftly and eagerly, excitedly returning home at the end of each day to describe to Taliya and her parents the wondrous things she was learning. She grew even further apart from all of the other children who had once been her playmates. Analya noticed the looks of fear and resentment they cast toward her and soon felt nothing but contempt for those who would not accept her. Often they threw small pebbles at her as she walked to her house or Taliya's, and she cried several times when remembering the happiness they had once shared. Each time, Taliya held her and dried her tears. "They're only jealous," she would tell Analya. "They are learning how to tend crops and make chairs, while you learn how to spin magical tales and spells."

When she was nine years old, Analya became an Apprentice Weaver. She moved out of her house and into the dormitory at the Weavers' Complex, where she continued her lessons, learning how to increase her control over her spells and the color and details of her Tales. However, she spent far more time studying alone with Malati, for her instructors had discovered that Analya was not only talented at Spellweaving and Taleweaving but that she had the talent for the third type of Weaving: Lifeweaving. Lifeweavers were incredibly rare, as rare among Weavers as Weavers were among all people. Malati taught Analya to sit before her loom and let her thoughts become still, sending her mind out into the world and weaving what she sensed. Malati also showed her how to follow a single thread through the pattern to see the life of a single person. Instead of focusing on a specific story and guiding her hands, as she did when she wove a Tale, Analya learned to let her hands guide themselves, weaving a pattern that only she and the other Lifeweavers could sense.

In her three years as an Apprentice, Analya seldom saw her parents and saw Taliya even less. During the times they could be together, Analya struggled to describe all that she was learning but found it more and more difficult to explain to those who simply couldn't see or sense what she could. Only Malati seemed to understand her frustration, and told Analya, "They're only threads, my dear. Only threads, winding their own solitary path. They cannot see the whole pattern, and there is no way you can make them see." Analya followed her mentor's advice and, for a while, stopped trying to explain to her parents and Taliya what she did in her studies. She listened to her father talk about his days making furniture and Taliya talk about her classes in history and government at school, but somehow she could not bring herself to see what caused their fascination in their chosen interests. They were so focused on their own lives, on their own interests. They could not see the pattern.

On her thirteenth birthday, Analya became a full Weaver. She removed the beads that formed her family's pattern from her necklace, leaving only the loom — the Weaver's charm — behind. As a Weaver, Analya was no longer part of a family, save that of the Weavers. Each morning she took her place at her loom, now in the Lifeweavers' Hall, and wove all day, recording the events that passed and the intertwining of the threads of life. The Hall was a pleasant room, full of sunlight from large windows during the day and a warm glow from Spell-lights as darkness fell. Analya spent her time contentedly Weaving, running her hands through the silky fibers, surrounded by threads of all possible colors.

In the evenings, before what the other Lifeweavers called the Untangling, she returned to her room and practiced her Taleweaving and Spellweaving; even Lifeweavers might need those skills someday. She asked the other Weavers about the Untangling, but even Malati would only say, "You'll be taught when you're ready." In addition to spending her free time Weaving, Analya spent many evenings with Malati, talking over mugs of hot cider or reading Tales. Over the years Analya had learned and lived in the Weavers' Complex, Malati had become her closest companion, simultaneously acting as a mentor, a mother, and a friend. Their difference in years didn't seem to matter; Analya was sure Malati understood her every action and thought. For the first time in her life, Analya felt she had a companion who saw the world from the same angle and through the same lens.

On the few occasions when she met with her parents and Taliya, Analya tried to describe her days and what she did. When Taliya asked about the Untangling, Analya simply replied that she didn't know. Taliya and her family seemed confused by her lack of knowledge, but she had long ago ceased to be concerned by their constant confusion about her talents and life. It didn't bother Analya; she was sure that Malati would tell her when the time was right.

One evening while Analya was contentedly Weaving a Tale that described her friendship with Taliya, someone knocked on her door.

"You have a visitor!" the Door Warden called. Confused, for she never had visitors, Analya opened the door. To her surprise, the Warden showed Taliya into Analya's room. Analya was shocked — neither her parents nor her friend had ever visited her at the Weavers' Complex; she always traveled to their houses. Then Analya realized that Taliya was tense and nervous, looking around as if she expected someone to leap out of the shadows and grab her.

"What's wrong?" Analya asked anxiously. "Why are you so upset?" Taliya didn't answer, continuing to stare around the room. Analya led her friend to her bed and, once she was sitting, covered her with a blanket describing a Tale of comfort and safety. Finally, Taliya began to speak.

"I've found out," she whispered. "I know about the Untangling. I know what it is." Suddenly, she jumped up, throwing off the blanket and grabbing Analya by the arm. "We have to go. We have to leave now. We have to get you out of here, get you away from these people and away from this place. I've talked to others, we're beginning to organize, we won't let this continue —"

Taliya stopped abruptly as Analya shook her hand off her arm. "What are you babbling about?" Analya cried angrily. "This place is my home, these people are my family, my friends." Then Analya stopped, and her anger grew cold. "I understand," she said coolly. "I see why you want to tear me away from my life. Just as you told me so many times, so many years ago . . . you're jealous. Jealous of what I have, of what I am, of what I can do, when you do nothing but sit in a school and study trivial subjects all day. I don't need you, and you have no right to take from me everything I love. Go back to those others you're friends with now, and don't bother me again."

At Analya's words, Taliya burst into tears and ran from the room. Analya could hear the Door Warden hurriedly opening the door below and letting Taliya out of the Complex. Analya turned to her bed, looking at the half-finished blanket she had been working on before Taliya came. With an angry gesture, she threw it under her bed and, as the tears started to fall, ran to Malati's room. Analya cried onto her mentor's shoulder, pouring out the entire story. With her vision blinded by tears, she didn't see Malati's eyes narrow when Analya described Taliya "organizing others." Malati held Analya until her tears stopped, all the while murmuring, "It's all right. It's all right. She's just jealous, she's just a thread, she doesn't understand. It's all right."

For two months, Analya threw herself into her work, Weaving

all day and then Weaving more at night, creating Spells and Tales until the walls of her room were covered in blankets, braids, chains, and knots. One day, as the sun was beginning to set, Malati stopped by Analya's loom.

"I'd like you to stay for the Untangling tonight," Malati said. "Is that a problem?"

"No, of course not!" Analya was barely able to contain her excitement. Finally, her teacher had deemed her ready to take the last step to being a true and full Lifeweaver. She finished her Weaving quickly and cleaned up. One by one, the other Weavers left their looms for the evening, until only she and Malati remained. They stood together, not talking, simply waiting. After a half hour, a man Analya had never seen before entered the Hall. Dangling from the chain around his neck were the Weaver's charm and another charm, the silver gavel that marked a government worker. He asked Analya to lead him to her loom, and when she did so he stood for a moment looking over the pattern.

"Very good," he commented. "You're very talented, for a Weaver so young." Analya blushed with pride and mumbled her thanks. "However," he continued, "there is one problem in your Weaving." He pointed to a snarl that Analya had first noticed about two months ago, which had continually grown larger and engulfed more and more threads each day.

"I know," Analya said, blushing again, this time with shame. "It won't seem to go away." At this, the man smiled.

"Don't be ashamed. It's not your fault," he replied. "That's the reason why we have Untanglings. Can you determine which thread is the core and the cause of the snarl?" Analya stared at the snarl, following its twists and turns in her mind, looking from every angle, until she finally discovered the thread that was the snarl's root. When she pointed it out, the man smiled once more.

"That's right. Taliya Brunati. Amazing, really. It's such a small, thin thread, no one would have expected it to cause the trouble that it has. But it's easily fixed," the man said as he handed Analya a small, glittering pair of scissors. She looked at him, aghast. "What are you waiting for?" he asked, his smile suddenly gone. "Untangle the snarl. Cut the thread out."

Analya stood stiff, unable to move. Her mind was racing, replaying for her all the happy scenes of her childhood, the times her friend had held her when she cried. Analya lifted her free hand in distress, toying with her necklace, feeling the chain devoid of the beads that marked her family allegiance and the single object hanging from it: her Weaver's charm. She thought of all the times she'd struggled to make her friend understand, without success. In her mind, Analya could see the crumpled, unfinished blanket still lying, dusty, beneath her bed.

She looked back to her loom, looked at the pattern and the threads. Suddenly, she understood the truth that had evaded her for so many years. She was a Lifeweaver, responsible for Weaving the threads of life. She didn't weave in response to what those threads did — those threads lived the pattern that she wove. It was not important that a single, narrow thread had been intertwined with her own for many years; she could look both within her own past and at the loom below her to see how far apart those two threads were now. Yet even if they were still intertwined, it would not matter. *She* was the Weaver. *She* controlled the loom, controlled the threads and their pattern. That single, insignificant thread was snarling the design and the government wanted it removed. Now, as she thought about it, her initial reaction to the man's request seemed downright silly. There was no reason to be bothered by such a logical request. Analya looked to Malati — her teacher, her mentor, her mother, her friend — and saw the confidence shining in her eyes.

Analya smiled, looking again at her loom. *After all, it's only a thread*, she thought to herself, and cut.

— Sarah Weiss

Just Another Excuse

in alphabetical order the poets sit
Lucille Clifton

Mark Doty
Marie Howe

Galway Kinnell

Yusef Komunyakaa

Sharon Olds
Robert Pinsky

Gerald Stern

and C. K. Williams
in alphabetical order they sit onstage

paying tribute to Stanley Kunitz
and I just keeping thinking

what if some crazy calls in a bomb threat?
a bomb threat

right here in Town Hall

the audience would be the first to panic
stuffy

gray-haired women
with handbags dangling at their sides

would push and shove
down the aisles toward the exit
frail men
with fat wallets

would chase after their wives
forgetting folded programs used as fans

the ushers
would lose control and burst from the theater
spitting curses at lectures and plays and concerts
saving their worst obscenities
for the poetry
that's keeping them away from their girlfriends
on this lonely Friday night

and maybe even a few oddballs
in the balcony
would leap wildly
over the metal railing
flying through the startled air
a couple skulls
cracking on the wooden armrests
of seats D3 and F8

but back onstage
the poets
superhuman and in alphabetical order
would remain calm
and Stanley Kunitz would come out
96 and blowing kisses
to the craziness
and if you'd look closely enough

you'd catch Robert Pinsky

        flashing a smile at Gerald Stern

and Yusef Komunyakaa

    sitting in peaceful meditation

and Marie Howe

    hunting through her red purse

for a pen

        this bomb threat

            just another excuse

    for a poem

— Eric Linsker

America: a Labor of Love Poem

America,
what happened to that girl I fell in love with at 4th of July parties
when I was too young to shoot fireworks?
I sat alone at the picnic table, sticky residue
of watermelon dried on my cheeks. I saw you standing there,
just as you were on Saturday morning cartoons, face to the Atlantic,
your schoolbooks in one hand, lollipop in the other.
You smiled blushingly at me from a screen and a flag
and I never knew what to say.

America,
when I was in high school, I wrote you a thousand love letters.
You never wrote back. I assumed the worse. I cut my hair
short, wore too much black, told everyone who asked
that you were a slut. I quit writing your name on every school
election ballot. I vandalized my history books. I wrote your name
in the boys' bathroom by the stairs. It was me who scrawled that note
about blow jobs next to a phone number.

America,
I'm sorry. I'm old enough now to know the difference
between a broken heart and a leaky faucet of hormones.
When I started college, I stopped carving your name
in every desk I sat in. I quit imagining you naked, one hand
on your hip, the other beckoning me with a thin finger
from the bedroom doorway. I hated you. I read

The Communist Manifesto more often than I read the Bible
or recited the pledge. Between the lines of every paper
I wrote was you: years spent calling a disconnected number,
years wasted talking to the same operator who was never you
and said she frankly couldn't give a shit less about the girl
I longed for, the girl who forgot to let the boys love her.

America,
I found you again in New York. You paused on the curb:
briefcase in one hand, relished hot dog in the other,
skirt hemmed three inches above your knees.
A Lucky Strike cigarette dangled between your lips.
To the huddled masses, you were just another girl-on-the-go,
but I knew better. To me, you were the girl I grew up
lusting after, the girl who grew up into something bigger
than me — a woman alone and content.

America,
you got old. You got bitter. You got ugly. For years,
I've watched you slip in and out of the public eye —
your starry dimples printed and burned on magazine covers.
That strong jaw dissolved into dentures, your nose twisted
too far to the right from too many incisions, surgeries, adjustments.

America,
I still go to church on Wednesday nights, even though
they've stopped praying for you. They pray for the president,
for the vice president, for the goddamn cabinet.
They don't pray for you because they know you trust

your well-being to prodigal sons. I pray for you, America.
I refuse to gossip about the way you're slipping and how far,
the way nurses and visitors run together in your eyes,
the way you've run out of money for prescriptions.
I want to write to you again, America. I want to believe
that maybe this time you'll respond, that maybe time
has forged a gap wide enough to piece this back together.

— Elbra Lillian Plott

Iraqi Boys Swimming

Their limbs stretch, muscles tight under tanned skin warm with sun.
In black shorts the boys fling themselves from the shore
arms spread as if they are flying.
One wears a white shirt, collar stretched to reveal a bird chest;
the fabric clings to his body, ribs dark wet outlines.

The Tigris swallows them whole as they weave their bodies in
and out of the jade water, toes kneading the warm mud of Baghdad.
Gazing at this magazine picture, glossy as though streaked with water or
    sweat,
I can imagine falling in love with the one on the far right —
his crooked grin, the soft arc of his golden back.

— Meghan Lee

Living Like That

1991: My cousin lets me try on his gas mask.

He laughs, of course, at the sight of my tiny eyes peering through a mass of twisted rubber. "And this is what you do when you get hungry," he explains, poking a tube into place somewhere near my mouth; he mimes slurping applesauce.

Words roll easily off his tongue — SCUD missiles, Patriots, warheads. He knows where the buckles and snaps fit on the mask, he knows how to unlock the vault-like metal door in his basement — the door to the *miklat*, the bomb shelter. We don't have one of those back home, just the television, where images of war play themselves out in surrealist waves of light. My seven-year-old mind associates missiles with spaceships and finds it entertaining to fire bars of green soap around the bathtub while I shout, "Here come the Patriots!" — words sounded out of a *Newsweek* cartoon. But my breath comes hot and close beneath the mask; his laughter sounds far off and flat as my small fingers fight to tear it off.

They said, even then, that you can't live in terror. You can't stop going outside, can't stop taking the nine o'clock bus to your office in Jerusalem because someone blew himself to pieces on it the morning you were home with the flu. You just can't live like that.

1996: A "suspicious package" is found on the corner of Ben Yehuda Street. Or in a taxi parked at the corner, I can't really tell from where I stand with my family behind police barricades, craning our necks with the other evacuated tourists. Bomb-sniffing dogs are brought. Robots. The package is someone's discarded lunch. We all breathe again.

Aliza Flatow has died. Back home, they name the parking lot for her. I watch helicopters from the beach; they mean something different to the people here.

I hear a joke: *An Israeli survived the Gulf War bombing of his apartment building and waited silently in rubble up to his neck for two days, till the rescue parties hauled him out, completely unscathed. Why didn't he scream for them? Because he couldn't move his hands!* I guess you had to be there.

1999: "I left it home this time," my grandmother tells the soldier, who grins down at her as he sifts through the jumbled contents of her handbag at the entrance to the shopping mall. He gets it and, with the machine gun on his back, can even find it funny.

You don't pick up hitchhiking soldiers anymore.

Our tour of the Jerusalem tunnels stops; there's a suspicious package up ahead. I blanch; my grandmother, amused by my American paranoia, assures me it's nothing, asks around for a bag for me to breathe into. The package is a bottle stuffed with wires. We run like hell for a taxi. She was right, though, it was nothing.

Cats scuffle in an aluminum trash can beneath the bathroom window, and I start, my half-combed hair standing on end in my wide-eyed reflection.

My carry-on is jerked from the X-ray conveyer belt by a strong, pink-polished brown hand, whose owner deposits it roughly on a side counter, waves an electronic wand over it, and toys with the zippers.

"What are you doing?" I demand. "What are you looking for?" She doesn't even look at me.

"Please," I beg a passing flight attendant, my fingers suddenly numb. "What's she looking through my bag for?"

The English is thick. "Plastic explosives." But she looks from the humiliated horror on my face to the UNACCOMPANIED MINOR sticker on my shirt, and in sharp Hebrew orders her partner to leave me, and my things, alone.

A bomb scare is the siren going off at three in the morning, and sliding gas masks over the faces of your wide-eyed, frightened children. It's mentally accounting, as someone once wrote to the *New York Times*, for each of your friends and loved ones every time the words "this just in" crackle from your radio. It's thinking, *Oh, my god, I was just there*. It's watching men from the *chevra kadisha* scrape human flesh from bloodstained light posts, so that bodies can be pieced back together and buried as whole as possible. It's knowing someone who knew someone who knew someone who. And it's crossing your fingers and going anyway.

— Esther Mittelman

I Kept Looking

I don't really remember that morning. The monotony of the commute was unremarkable in and of itself on the second day of our first full week of school. Perhaps the dreadful normality of that morning makes everything all the worse. I probably talked to some friends, did some unfinished homework. Not thinking about anything in particular, I just let myself be carried beneath the city. Sometimes on the subway I feel the proximity of people very strongly, and the strangeness of traveling like this, and the industrial grandeur of these underground trains. But probably not on that sleepy morning.

If I look hard enough at something, I often find that I am fascinated and frightened by it. No matter what I see, I can find something larger than myself hidden in it. This is a peripheral sensation for me, an intellectual response to the subject. I can easily become engrossed in the most trivial things, spending hours looking at the different ways that a wave can crash against rocks, imagining the awesome power of the sea, and wondering what is just over the blue rim at the edge of my vision. Here, I have a strong feeling of some greater entity, of some bigger force in the world, of a thing more important and larger than myself. Even by just describing this and remembering again this thing, I feel the tingle of the unknown, and the tightness of anxiety. However, there are so many things that can elicit this response from me, to a greater or lesser degree, that I feel I need to search for something deeper, a moment when I felt that my life was changing. Reading a well-written book sometimes puts me into a state removed from the larger reality but awed by what I have just finished. I could be walking down Park Avenue when I suddenly notice how tall the buildings really are, and how many people there are, and how if I turn fully around I can see four concrete ravines leading to the encircling horizon, that I feel alone, and feel the presence of something else.

After fourth period, nobody even thought of going back to class. There were nondescript, fuzzy announcements on the PA system. I don't remember walking to pick up my sister, but next thing I knew, I was with her, calling home. I got a busy signal every time. I walked with a false sense of purpose and looked for people I knew. I escaped the nervous chaos of the school hallway and was offered a lift home.

The five of us — myself, my sister, Jane, Simone, and Nell — were waiting on the southeast corner of Ninety-fourth and Park, waiting for Jane's dad to pick us up. We had all taken the bus together in elementary school, and that commute had almost always been exciting and different. Or at least I remembered it that way. It was now early afternoon, and the sun was warm as we sat against a building. The air was quiet and hung loosely on everything around. There were few cars on the streets to break the silence.

Of course, we first talked about where we were when we had heard the news, what we had thought, what happened next. But humor seems to come naturally at the oddest moments. We joked about our new teachers. One had a lisp. One gave too much homework. "Look, we have to read all of these pages in the new art textbook!" Someone giggled at a picture of a nude in a painting. "I'm going to be up all night finishing this reading!" Simone laughed too loudly. Jane laughed too quietly. I tried to laugh, but couldn't force it out. My sister held my hand tightly.

But I felt the same as I had when I got up that morning. The sky was the same piercing blue as it must have been when I walked to the subway station. I stood up at the base of our concrete canyon and climbed into Jane's dad's car, which had just arrived.

Perhaps I hold everything at arm's length, observing from far away, perhaps afraid of the indefinite, but always equally entranced — a defense mechanism of sorts. I find that often it is easier to withdraw from something that is larger than myself, easier to deal with if I don't get caught up in it. I can witness life through a defensive window, but I don't think I want to. I fantasize about living a secluded life, perhaps a hermit's life, where I can always keep these things at arm's length and never really let them get to me deeply, but where I can appreciate what is around me. Where I can think abstractly and play with thought experiments and where I don't have to get swept up in anything if I don't want to. What I have noticed, even writing this rambling exploration, is that being alone has a great deal to do with this sense of something bigger. A cold winter night on a deserted street makes me feel small and alone and forces me to think about things larger than myself; reading a book is a solitary enterprise, and noticing how you yourself have changed is an experience entirely encapsulated by yourself. But I can keep these things away and let the feeling into my consciousness a little bit at a time; I can protect myself from the unknown.

*　　*　　*

On the way downtown, we listened to the radio. I looked out the window, noticing the sights familiar from the days of my school bus. We had the radio on, and Jane's dad kept up a one-sided conversation. The radio talked about Pearl Harbor and sounded unreal. "This day will live in infamy," they said, quoting Roosevelt.

"Roosevelt didn't say that. That was Churchill." I hadn't actually been listening. "Winston Churchill: 'This day will live in infamy.' World War Two. Why do they have to mix these things up?" Jane's dad continued his conversation. I had thought it was really Roosevelt, but I didn't say anything. I just looked out the window, this time looking toward the front windshield instead of out my side window.

"You see that cloud?" I did. There was one large cloud directly south of us. Like a large thunderhead building in the afternoon sky, I had thought.

"You know what that is, don't you?" I really didn't know what he was talking about. It just looked like a cloud to me. I thought he had to be even more tense than any of us.

"That's all that's left of them."

We were stopped by police barricades at Fourteenth Street, but since we lived farther down, they let us continue south. We were stopped again at Houston Street. No cars below Houston. The only sounds were the moaning of sirens. There were only people below Houston, confused humanity, and they were moving in only one direction. We walked against the tide, toward home.

I had once seen a ticker-tape parade when the Yankees won

121

the World Series, and there had been so much confetti that I could barely make out some of the buildings downtown. The confetti had floated gently up and down, looking like so many falling petals. Now there was so much smoke and dust that I couldn't see any of the buildings, and a sandstorm right out of the *Arabian Nights* seemed to have blanketed the area. And the smell. An acrid stench choked the neighborhood. The smoke of the fires, the dust of the buildings, the bones of the dead. The smell bit at your nose and reminded you constantly, just in case you might have forgotten. Six months later, you could still smell it if the wind was right, and it would always make me pause midstep. Then I would walk out the door and continue with my daily life.

Sometimes I want to travel the world and do nothing but observe. I want to learn every language, I want to visit every place, I want to know every person's story, and I don't ever want to forget. And I don't know why, because that scares me. Would I like to be a modern explorer, a modern nomad, a modern man living outside the present? I do and I don't. For that would represent the last stage in separating myself from the fabric of the world, as if I were on the moon and looking at all these places through a telescope. I would get a sense of the location, but I would be outside of the action.

Despite these funny daydreams of mine, I don't want to be alone.

The television was on when I got home, competing with the sirens. I went to sleep with the television on that night, and I woke up with it on the next morning. My parents had seen one of the planes hit. They had seen the towers collapse. My clever dad had predicted they would collapse. He had taken two rolls of film and a video of the entire event. He gave me a scratchy dust mask with yellow elastic bands. I was to wear that. We didn't know what was in the smoke. Who knows what the terrorists had brought on the planes with them? I went to sleep later with the mask on, too.

"I heard a loud thundering, and the whole building shook as the plane went by," my dad said. "*ZZHHEEWWWW*. It was that loud."

I went onto the roof.

I sat on the fire escape by myself and watched the smoke gently twist up and away; I watched the constantly changing patterns in the dust, the delicate swirls and eddies. The serpentine smoke climbed up and twisted and contorted itself. I couldn't even imagine where the towers had been. I kept looking south for a long time, just sitting alone in the sunlight.

Later, my family went for a walk around SoHo, and we met with our neighborhood friends. The streets were deserted except for us, and no one was walking north anymore. The little kids played ball, running up and down and shouting happily. There were the shouts, and the sirens, and the burning smell. There was a thin haze hanging over the street, and we walked in the middle of the road. I was breathing in the World Trade Center. There was a fine ash on the fire hydrants, a thin coating of dust. I kept glancing downtown, then slowly looking back.

"I remember when SoHo used to be like this," my dad said. "No cars. I wish it was still like this." I felt like hitting him. That night, I cried myself to sleep for the first time in years.

There are things larger than myself similar to ones I have

already described. But the most important, the ones that change your whole outlook, the events that alter you as a person and touch you deeply and emotionally are events that you cannot hold at arm's length. They are things that carry you up and away, that occupy your mind without thought of anything else. They are things that you can't distance yourself from. And while I didn't really want to write about this subject, I almost feel obligated to because there has never been anything in my life that fits these criteria better. For me the most powerful and significant of these events is September 11.

A year afterward, I sat in the courtyard and remembered. I felt tears running down my cheeks, and again I let myself cry. I felt sorry for those who, with typical cynicism, had forgotten, or who pretended they had forgotten.

— Alexander Fabry

There Is Nothing So Red as Cranberry Juice

There is nothing so red as cranberry juice
Nothing so pale as your eyes.
I've seen nothing so green as a green jelly bean
And nothing so frail as these skies.

— Ian Ferguson

To My Twin Brother Who Died at Birth

On the ferry into Halifax,
the folds of the palsied sea
shine cold and black
as wet wind snatches at our hair but we
are shadows sharing a broken
deck chair in the fog, silent,
breathing in salt air and cigarette smoke
in the moonless dark. The sea tosses, violent
thrashings and the crush and roar
of water. I can easily forget
that I knew you before
cold, before light —
Waves slap the hull, breaking in a hiss
of foam — there is no hollowness like this.

— Hallie Rundle

Eryk

Every Christmas morning,
my grandfather opens a bright,
papered box of Smirnov Vodka,
its bottle the color of the snowy,
rolling fields from home.

One single shot and he's back.
His wife is baking a rye loaf,
while he blows on a piece
of kielbasa he has bitten off
for his daughter.

He stays only long
enough to recall faces
that soil and time
have withered away.
They become nameless,
numberless victims.

From the refuge of his chair,
he tells me a story,
about guarding livestock
from skeletal wolves
that howled and slipped
from drift to drift
like spectral madmen.

That afternoon I see him
delicately crumbling
fruitcake for stray birds,
penitent old man.

— Jennifer Holcombe

Water Washes It Away with the Dirt

I always wanted my mother to tell me
what she saw appealing in Poppa
why she stayed with him for so long
why she loved him so hard
he took her across the country
nothing fast and amazing
like a *Bean Trees* road trip
he snatched her still dirty
knocked her up three times
and she kept silent still

but I hear her at night
alone in our carpeted kitchen
her chest heaving

I always wanted my mother to tell me
how she knew that baking soda
makes everything clean
she sprinkles it on sidewalks
rubs it on her toothbrush
and water washes it away with the dirt

— Mary Brady

What Cancer Meant

List

He had tumors. He had them all over, but the ones that killed him were on his spine. After he was diagnosed, he had four years to live. He had seven surgeries. He had chemotherapy and radiation: Leukovorin, 5FU, CPT-11, Oxaliplatin.

He had medical tests. He had biopsies, MRIs, CAT scans, PET scans, X-rays. He got his results — large pictures of the inside of his body always came in the same oversize tan envelope.

He had doctors. He had oncologists and ophthalmologists, surgeons, neurologists, gastroenterologists, and radiologists. The doctors varied in degrees of competency and friendliness. He had technicians who gave him his test results and doctors who interpreted them. He had three different hospitals in three different towns in three different states. He received late-night phone calls and different treatment suggestions. Sometimes he had false hope.

He had friends, a wife, and three children. He had co-workers and students. Because of this, he received cards and good wishes. Prayers were said for him. He received casseroles and cakes and phone calls and presents and hugs and hands to hold and tears.

He had different moods — thankful and hopeful and affectionate and angry and helpless and despairing.

He had the sharp pain from the tumors just under his skin like a cigarette being put out on his back. He had the deeper, duller pain from the tumors inside. He had headaches and muscle aches. He had a cough that rattled drily. He had a sore throat and stomach cramps. He had only one good eye left. He had cancer, which was every illness — fatigue and the flu and migraines and kidney stones — all rolled into one.

He had painkillers: Percocet, Darvon, Ativan, Oxycontin, and morphine. He had prescriptions written for anything in a tiny bottle that might do the trick. He had marijuana. He had rented hospital equipment. He had his own hospital bed and later, when he lost use of his legs, a cane, a walker, then a wheelchair.

He had memories — a trip to the Grand Canyon, Key West, a beach house, reading a newspaper, eating breakfast, his drive to work, training a puppy, mowing the lawn, talking on the phone, a movie, a book, a song. He had broken dreams — he knew he would not see his children's graduations or weddings or first homes or his first grandchild. He had realized dreams. He had traveled, had taught math, had a family. He had a life. And he had tumors.

Breathe

He is dying.

You know that the minute you walk through the front door. The air in your house is full of death. It carries a smell that you have come to recognize as fear. And in the past few months, the members of your family have become obsessed with the concept of death — reading books, discussing it endlessly, trying to make some sense of where your father is going, trying desperately to understand this final life process. In your house it is hard to complain, not about the fact that your mother insists you not miss a day of school, not about the constant ache that comes from somewhere deep inside of you. In your house, things have been reduced to merely being grateful that you are not dying.

Your mother stops you before you enter the bedroom at the back of your house. She says, Before you go in there I just want to prepare you. Things are happening very fast. It doesn't look good. You can go in, but I don't want you to be surprised.

So you go in and try not to be surprised at the fact that your father in his hospital bed at the side of the room already looks like a corpse. His skin is pale yellow and there is nothing but bones underneath. He breathes noisily through his open mouth. One eye cannot close all the way. But the skin over his forehead is smooth — no wrinkles, no signs of distress or strain.

The hospital bed is a few inches away from the big double bed that used to belong to both your parents but is now just your mother's bed. You lie down on the bed and stretch out on your back. You try to climb down from the high tower in which you have placed yourself. This is my father, you remind yourself. The man in the rented hospital bed is not a stranger. This is your father. So you will stay. No parties no friends no homework no phone calls no food no sleep. You will stay.

Your mother looks ready to take a welcome respite from the job of watching over your father all day, but at the same time she looks unable to drag herself away even for a hurried dinner. You feel the same conflict of instincts. You want desperately to run out of this room, away from this man with the sharp bones and yellow skin. But at the same time you know that nothing, nothing in the entire world could make you leave.

You stare at the ceiling. You unintentionally begin to breathe in the same rhythm as your father, matching the timing of each breath to his. His breathing has become shallow—quick gulps of air spaced very far apart. You wonder if by breathing at the same time you can both somehow lower yourselves into peace. You have one wish. You want more than anything you've ever wanted in your life to take his pain, just take a little of it for yourself, to lessen his burden in any way you can. Every chance you get, you pray to a God you've stopped believing in: Please, God, just let me take some of the pain. But God doesn't listen, and you know that when your father wakes up from this morphine-induced sleep, all the pain will be waiting for him again.

Your father wakes. You know this by the change in his breathing: rapid, more agitated. You sit up quickly. His eyelids flicker slightly. Your muscles tense, fight-or-flight kicking in. You will stay. You will stay. He is beyond speaking, beyond immediately recognizing who is in the room with him. And then he is asleep again.

Yesterday he had been full of talk when he was awake. His descriptions of his morphine-inspired dreams fell in a steady stream on your mother's ears. At the end of each description your father smiled slightly and shook his head and said, I'm hallucinating. She also told you about the middle of last night, when he woke and tossed and turned and spoke what will prove to be his last words: Help me. Help me.

And now he is sleeping and silent. He is someplace else. As his pain becomes greater, he spends more and more time in another world. You watch as his forehead smooths itself out again and you wonder where he goes, what he sees. Flashes of the world, perhaps: a river, a baseball diamond, a rock, a street, a cave. A cloud, a snowstorm, a fire truck, his doctors now checking over their new patients. Your mother. You.

And so you lie on that bed, breathing in the rhythm he has given you, and you know that in the coming hours, one by one, your mother and brother and sister will join you. And when the four of you sit on your mother's bed, your father's rhythm will change. And you will know. And the four of you will stand around him, your mother holding his right hand and you holding his left, and he will leave you. And though it will be a moment so powerful that you won't even realize it while it is happening, there will be a small relief because your one wish will have been granted. You will carry his pain with you, with the memory of his bones solid and sure under his skin, in some sacred corner of your heart.

The Book for the Dead

There is a road I can follow that will take me to you.

But it is not an easy road, and I cannot go there often. The concentration it requires is an immense undertaking unlike any other. There are no obstacles in the way when I try to follow this road, but there are so many branches, so many side paths. To keep following the main road I must be committed. I must give everything: my mind, my heart, my soul.

To lapse in the intense thought process, the huge psychological strain, is so tempting. And then I will stray from the main road and end up following one of the easier side paths. Once I do that, it is better if I had not started on the journey at all.

I remember the first time I realized I could do this — that I had the power to visit the world of the dead. I was in bed at night. I could feel the tug on the cord that still connects my soul to your soul. Closing my eyes, I began to follow the cord, mapping out the road I discovered as I went. The scenery surrounding the road is not such that we can perceive it with our ordinary senses. But if I had to describe it to someone who hasn't traveled it, I would say that it looks like being in the middle of a falling snow against a black sky. And there is the sense of speed. Stars? Another universe?

And then, as my physical body tired and feel asleep, I arrived. My first glimpse of the world of the dead was big blue sky. I was floating on my back in what felt like water. The ocean. The ocean on a beautiful day. I could not see you, but you were there. And already the mental concentration was taking its toll, and I could feel myself being pulled back into the physical world. I could still think in words. (Words have never deserted me.) And I thought, I have time for one question. Just one question.

Well, what does it feel like to be dead? I asked you.

First it feels like this. I did not hear your voice but I knew what you had said. The waves in the ocean began to increase until there was one big wave, one giant leap, one jump, one sudden setting free. *Then it feels like this.* And the waves returned to their gentle rocking. Suddenly my eyes snapped open and I was back home in the world of the living. Outside my window the sun was coming up. It had taken me the entire night to travel so far.

And that was the first of perhaps three other meetings. Although I have tried nearly every night, it is only rarely that I am able to traverse the great distances. The later meetings were clearer than the first. Sometimes I can see you and touch you and hear your voice just as I would in the physical world. After the first time you must have discovered how to make it easier for me.

Whenever we meet I always want to talk about you and you always want to talk about me. Once we had had a very long conversation; I only remembered a few sentences of it when I woke up. You always seem so concerned. You want to know how I am doing, how I am getting along without you. On the night before your funeral service, you gave me a lecture. You told me that I'd soon need to be very strong. You must have known what would happen the next day.

I'm afraid that when I die I won't see you, I said once. I'm afraid that you're going to be reincarnated before I can come join you.

You don't need to worry about that, you told me. *I'm not going to be reincarnated. That's only if your soul is at a certain level.*

What level are you at? I asked.

Well, you said, with the tone of humility just touched with pride that you used so often in life, *I am at the highest level.*

And once, in the best meeting, my favorite meeting, we cried together. That's all we did, just cry, for I don't know how long, the whole night maybe. I remember that we tried to just talk but we really missed each other too much. And you were holding me on your lap like you did when I was a child, and I could feel your arms around me, really truly feel them. And we were both sobbing. That was our most honest, least formal meeting. And, for some reason, the easiest one for me to stay in.

Sometimes when I try to get to you, when I try to arrive in the land of the dead, I take a detour along the way. It's such an amazing thing, to be able to travel to the world of the dead, and sometimes my fear diverts me. Then I am confronted with my own recollections of you right before you died, not quite reaching my true vision of you after your death. It's so hard then, even though I know that they are only dreams.

In my dreams you die again. And then I move into another dream in which you die. I can't bear to watch you die so many times. Sometimes I forget that this story always has the same ending, and I talk to you, lying there on your bed. I say, Don't worry, Daddy, you are not going to die this time. I promise that you are not going to die. Sometimes you believe me, but you always die anyway. In my dreams I cannot stop you from dying, even though you are supposed to be able to do anything in dreams.

Sometimes, in the dreams, I am alone with you and I realize you are dying. I don't know what to do so I run and try to find Mom. When I come back you have died already, and I feel so terrible that I let you die alone. I am as helpless in my dreams as I am in real life. So sometimes, fearful of another dream, I don't try to visit the world of the dead at all. I fall asleep reciting chemistry equations instead.

Sometimes it is strange because I am the only one in our family with the ability to travel to the world of the dead. I have told Mom and Jenna and Sam, and they believe me and are comforted. They don't have to deal with my insecurities, my feeling that I am making a reality out of a fantasy. And they don't have to keep getting diverted and reliving your death. It's so strange, living with one foot in each of two different worlds. I am waiting to return to the living. I am waiting to die.

And the cord that connects us pulls and pulls, creating such pain right in the middle of my chest. It makes me feel your absence all the more, but sometimes it can lead me to you. And if I just follow it, and try my best not to ignore what it tells me, I know I will arrive anywhere with safety, protected by forces greater than I am. When you were alive this cord didn't hurt so much, but it's always been there, probably ever since I first saw you, since I first entered the world of the living. I don't need to tell you the rest. You already know what makes up the cord — you already know how we are connected.

I love you, Dad.

— Katrina Gersie

5 Shot, 3 Dead in Whidbey Murder-Suicide
June 20, 2002

I was seven years old when I first met my cousin Holly. The rental car had barely come to a halt in front of my uncle's house when we were mobbed by seven of his kids.

"Do you wanna ride bikes?"
"Do you wanna watch *Ninja Turtles*?"
"Do ya got any candy?"

My mom gave me an understanding *well, here we are* look and we headed inside. That's when I saw Holly, the eighth cousin. She was at the kitchen counter, making herself a peanut butter and honey sandwich. She was the only one who seemed unaffected by our visit. Holly seemed unaffected by everything. Even as her mom scolded her for leaving gobs of gooey honey on the counter, she simply picked up her sandwich and walked outside, leaving the amber goo for a community of black ants, already beginning to form at the pool's edge.

ISLAND COUNTY — A 23-year-old man shot his fiancée and her mother to death and wounded two other people before turning the gun on himself Thursday, the Island County sheriff said.

My sisters and girl cousins played She-Ra that afternoon. We boys barged in to prove our mettle, but even He-Man needs to pee sometimes. As I looked out the tiny bathroom window, I noticed Holly, perfectly framed by the window's wooden border, dwarfed by the Silver Tree and weaving a chain of wildflowers. Perhaps she was weaving it as a crown for the Lady of the Golden Wood. She seemed more connected to the fairies.

About 18 shotgun shells littered the road in the small subdivision on the southern end of Whidbey Island, about 28 miles north of Seattle.

I don't think that I even spoke to Holly on that visit, except to maybe say, "Please pass the ketchup" or "Would you like a black jelly bean?" Money and distance prevented me from seeing my cousins very often, but for the next few Christmases, a 5 x 7 photograph would come in the mail, along with the Monnett Family Newsletter. The photo had to be 5 x 7 my aunt said, because eight kids can't fit on a 3 x 5. I never read the newsletters, or even asked about them, but I did look at the photographs. It seemed to me that Holly always stood just a few inches away from the other cousins.

Deputies responding to a report of gunfire found the bodies of Marjorie Monnett, 55, of Freeland, and her daughter, Holly Monnett-Swartz, 24, of Clinton, in the street in front of Monnett's home. Monnett-Swartz's fiancé, Preston Dean "Hugh" Douglas, 23, of Clinton, was found dead on top of her, Sheriff Michael A. Hawley said.

On the third Christmas after our visit, the Monnett Family Newsletter arrived, but no photo was included. My parents' hushed tones alerted me to something mysterious going on. I asked my big sister if Uncle Jack and Aunt Marjie were getting a divorce. "It's bigger than that," she said. "Holly ran off with a motor-cycle gang!" As an impressionable ten-year-old, that sounded pretty cool to me. I didn't understand why all the shock and shame was attached to Holly heading off on an adventure. I didn't know that the honey-gobber flower weaver had been gang raped and left on the street.

There was no previous history of abuse in the home, and no one involved had a criminal history, Sheriff Hawley said. Monnett-Swartz had recently taken a job at the Good Cheer thrift shop in nearby Langley. Douglas, a Jamaican national and unemployed landscaper, had been babysitting for the girl.

By the fourth Christmas my family had saved up enough money to visit my mom's brother again. I had never seen snow before and the visit was to cold country. I was looking forward to a white Christmas probably even more than spending it with the Monnett family. Things always seemed a little unsettling to me at my aunt and uncle's house. In my family, Christmas presents were put under the tree and looked at (with an occasional poke or shake) with great longing and anticipation until Christmas Day. At my uncle's house, presents were kept under lock and key in a specially made cupboard. My cousins secretly showed me how to remove the door brackets with a screwdriver while still keeping the lock in place. We had unwrapped and rewrapped every present several times before Christmas morning. Labels were replaced haphazardly. In one covert operation, I unwrapped a gift labeled with my name. My cousins laughed hysterically as I held up a baby blanket and something called a layette. I didn't see Holly that Christmas, but shortly after we arrived back home, a baby announcement came in the mail.

The day before, Monnett-Swartz called the sheriff's office to say she thought Douglas had molested her daughter two weeks ago, Hawley said. An investigator suggested she move out of the residence she shared with him in Clinton, and she did — moving in with her mother Wednesday night.

Holly seemed to settle down for a little while after Sage was born. I don't know if Sage was named for wisdom or for the medicinal herb, but she did seem to have a soothing effect on Holly. It was shortly after Sage's birth that Holly married a truck driver named Swartz. The family thought that maybe it would all work out in the end. One night Holly showed up at my aunt and uncle's house. She was beaten up real bad. She had Sage with her and said that she was never going back.

Less than 24 hours later, Douglas arrived armed with a 12-gauge, pistol-grip shotgun, his pockets full of shotgun shells packed with birdshot. He walked through the woods and entered the family's home through a back door.

I didn't see Holly again until the beginning of last summer. We had a big family reunion up at Brian Head. Uncle Jack had rented a cabin that slept about a hundred people. All of the cousins were there — single, married, and otherwise. One night in the kitchen I asked Holly if she was happy. She showed me the eight-inch butterfly tattooed between her shoulder blades and gave me a big grin. Everybody said that she had met a real nice guy and was going to be getting married again.

Hawley gave this account: Douglas parked his rusty, light blue van about 50 yards from the home at about 1:30 a.m. He walked in the back door and shot Bruce Monnett in the kitchen. Monnett's girlfriend ran to the garage, where Douglas shot her, nearly severing her arm. Monnett, soaked with blood from a gunshot wound to the stomach, ran to a neighbor's house. Neighbors who watched through the windows reported seeing Douglas going from room to room, apparently looking for Monnett-Swartz, who was at a house two doors down.

If the high altitude and mountain air agreed with Holly, then it was downright euphoric for Sage. Every afternoon she would beg me to take her on a walk. She really didn't have to beg too hard. She was pretty cool for a six-year-old. She'd climb on my back and pretend to be a fairy princess. She loved picking wildflowers. When we'd get back, she'd always give her mom a bouquet.

Monnett-Swartz's 6-year-old daughter knew where her mother was and ran there unharmed. Douglas started to follow, firing a shot in the air and yelling for Monnett-Swartz. That's when Mrs. Monnett ran out into the street. He shot her in the hip and, after she collapsed, in the head. Monnett-Swartz, watching from inside a neighbor's house, came outside. She too was

shot in the hip and then in the face. Douglas approached her body and shot himself in the head, crumpling on top of her.

The neighborhood association president, Al Thomas, was asked what he planned to do to help the neighbors cope with the slayings. "I haven't even thought about that," he said shortly after the crime-scene tape came down and neighbors were allowed out of their homes. "Everybody has their own way of grieving."

— Ashton Alvarez

Mother, When We Were Young

Memory stopped me beneath a tree one night during a lone walk across November's hoarfrost fields. In the west the last shreds of orange light were draining from the ground's white salting. Eastward the stars glimmered coldly, their sky a flux of darkness riding on purple twilight. The weight of the books on my back had pulled me to a halt before I had reached the hill in front of my dormitory, and as I shifted my shoulders to find a soft couch for the biting straps, I thought of my mother. I thought of the September day we parted, standing side by side on the threshold of my new life, and of the suitcases that had bent her small frame double as she insistently dismissed my soft-armed attempts to intervene and heaved the bags by herself up all four flights of the dormitory stairs.

When I was young, in our early years in China, she used to secure me to a straw basket on the back of her bicycle, and after art lessons and piano lessons on Sunday mornings we would head to an expensive sundae parlor for my single scoop of vanilla ice cream with bitter chocolate sauce on top. (In China, it cost a day's salary from a teacher's pocketbook.) I still recall the delicate lace of dark sweetness against icy white, the exquisite little-girl glamour of eating from porcelain at snowy-linened tables, and the selfish way I licked clean the spoon. I can almost hear again the musical clink of silverware and the purl of conversation all around as my mother sat with her arms folded in her lap, still as a stone in eddying water, watching with a content smile my attack upon the coveted delight. When I had finished, we left the glittering confines of the restaurant and I climbed ably into the straw basket. She would then take out an old handkerchief embroidered with her childhood and wipe the corners of my lips where the guilty aftertaste of imported chocolate still lingered in brown traces, and the cocoa perfume of one day's salary, one day in front of a dusty chalkboard. The coarse handkerchief was rough against my baby-haired skin. Sometimes she wetted it with her tongue before dabbing at my pouted mouth.

It was she who taught me gratitude: its invisible silk ropes that bind one human being to another, its dull brown lace of bitterness and sweetness, its aftertaste of residual sorrow, its infinite debt, its lifetime interest. She was the one who taught me always to write Thank-You notes (and Merry Christmas, and Happy Easter, and Have A Joyful Thanksgiving This Year And Always From All of Us In Appreciation), my masterpieces the culmination of a third-grader's laborious cursive inked out painstakingly across thirsty blank notes with flowers blooming on the covers. Thank You to my teachers who taught me how to wield a pen, Thank You to my American grandparents who took us into their home, Thank You to my piano teacher who taught me every Sunday morning free of charge, Thank You to the institutions that paid for my education, Thank You Thank You Thank You (and even if my heart is ripped asunder leaking this breathless two-word prayer it shall never suffice to pay the cost of gratitude, or ease its perpetual weight). She taught me by example, her own weary face slipping into shadows behind a smiling mask with which she fronted the world. Her capacity for gratitude was my inheritance.

With her reflexive gratefulness also came a strange, fine, tender pride, compressed deep inside her passionate humility like obsidian rock, the metamorphic product of our hard-won first years in America. Out of this pride sprang limitations. There were people to whom we would never express our true opinions (much more polite to mind your own business); people to whom a child should never display her smarts (a full bottle makes no sound while a half-full bottle makes a lot of rattle); people to whom we would always give the right of way; people who bound her to them through kindnesses she could not afford. In our early years in this country she waitressed at the Notre Dame University dining hall by day, studying for her master's degree by night, to make ends meet. Every gesture of giving she tried to deserve, even when the gift was hers to keep. This was the economy of her heart.

Standing here in cold clarity, Mother, seventeen years old, a girl who is earning her right to leave some Thank Yous left unvoiced and tucked inside the chrysalis of mutual understandings, I remember clearly your aching arms. I remember your hours of grace, your sacrifices manifold, the years of a paralyzing gratitude and their toll on your strength. I remember your pilgrim spirit. I envision you now standing unfettered, straight as a tree in a lone field on a winter night, head arched brightly toward the stars. And I tug at the lassos that bind me to you, and you to the world. My fingers curl around the knots in my throat and worry them gently one strand at a time, kneading and straining in the hope that one day I can make you proud, and we can set each other free.

— Baolu Lan

Manchurian Girl

"Why do you bother?" he asks for the millionth time in a sneering tone.

"Because . . ." I shrug lightly, not wanting to tell him, not wanting to talk about it.

But he's too persistent for a vague answer like that. "Why do you try so hard? What's your motivation for getting good grades and stuff? Taking classes like calculus?"

"Dunno. Why do *you* try so hard, Mr. Sophomore French AP?" I retort, hoping he would leave me alone.

He doesn't. Instead, he changes the subject. "Know what I heard a Japanese police chief say once?"

"What?" I ask flatly. Not because I'm interested, but because he's going to say whatever it is anyway.

"Rape is unfortunate, but it happens, so when it does, the women should just try to let go and enjoy themselves." He laughs with a glint in his eye.

I clench the straps of my backpack to restrain myself from slapping him across the face. "Okay," I reply as calmly as possible before walking away. "Bastard," I mutter under my breath. He's one of those cocky chauvinists who scorn any guy who can't score 1500 on the SAT . . . and any girl who *can*. I think his feud with me started when I beat him on a math test by about two points (when I wasn't even trying to compete with him). It wouldn't have been a big deal except for two things: I'm a girl, and he's Chinese. Not watered-down, fifth-generation half Taiwanese, half Caucasian, either. Purebred Sichuan, central Yangtze, born and raised.

Those two facts don't seem like much unless you're from mainland China. I'm not talking about places like Beijing or Shanghai, either. Those cities don't count, because they're large and cosmopolitan and westernized. When I say mainland China, I mean somewhere away from the harbors, where the street signs don't have English translations for tourists, where the hotels don't have clocks at the registration desk showing Tokyo and Paris times, and where the concept of feminism doesn't exist. I'm from one of those places. So is he. And one of the ugliest aspects of mainland China is the lack of respect for women.

The answer to his question — "Why do you bother?" — is very long and complicated, or maybe very short and simple. I don't know. It's rooted in the Manchurian traditions in which I was brought up and against which I have been rebelling for fifteen years. The ironic thing is that he should know the answer to his own question better than almost anyone else. He's Chinese enough to understand.

My father was the oldest of three sons. He had a sister, too, but girls didn't matter in northeastern China, where my father's family came from. So we can ignore my aunt and her daughter, my older cousin, because they didn't exist on our family tree. My grandmother had only three children, all of them sons.

I was the firstborn in the family. The doctors were not allowed to tell my mother beforehand if I was a boy or girl. In an attempt to control the burgeoning population, the Chinese government had passed a law limiting most families to one child (twins, triplets, etc., were perfectly fine, of course). Any pregnancies after that had to be aborted (the abortions were generously funded by the state).

Many women who knew they were pregnant with girls had abortions, often dangerous and illegal ones. In the remote countryside, where government officials and hospitals were scarce, many newborns ended up at the bottom of a river, wrapped in blankets that doubled as funeral shrouds. Those babies were always female. So doctors stopped telling prospective mothers the baby's gender. Sometimes I wonder what would have happened if some doctor had said to my parents, "It's a girl," but maybe questions like that are better left unasked.

When I turned out to be a girl, my grandmother was furious. Her eldest son, a prestigious Ph.D. from Tsinghua (the most prominent university in the country), the pride and joy of her life, was stuck with a daughter, with no chance of ever having a son to pass on the family name, or honor, or whatever it was that a boy child was supposed to do. A girl could only do housework, get married, and bear sons for *another* family. As far as my grandmother was concerned, I would be a waste of time and money.

But my mother didn't give up on me. Maybe because she was from Jiangxi, in the south, and people there didn't believe girls were quite as useless as Manchurians did. She spent every spare moment she had teaching me everything she could, from music theory to arithmetic. Maybe she, too, wanted to prove to her patriarchal in-laws that not all girls were worthless.

I don't think my grandmother (or anyone else on my father's side, for that matter) took much interest in me until I was three or four. Maybe I understood at some level, even then, that I had something to prove. Whenever I visited my grandmother's house, I had to strike a delicate balance between showing off everything I knew and acting like the demure, obedient child that every

Chinese girl was supposed to be. I think when I finally achieved that balance, my grandmother started to love me. She pointed me out to her neighbors and made me demonstrate the three hundred Han characters I could read and write by age three. I was worth something after all.

I had worked hard to earn my love. Unconditional love only existed for boy children. I found that out when my first cousin was born. Everyone was ecstatic because it was a boy. My aunt crowed with joy and turned her nose up at my mother, who had no son. I watched the baby with childish hatred and jealousy. The attention and care naturally lavished on the pink, wiggling mass was more than I had ever gotten. While my uncle dragged his brothers and friends out to celebrate by getting drunk, I madly practiced scales on the piano, more determined than ever to prove that I was as intelligent and useful as any boy.

When I was seven, my family moved to America. I left behind the grandparents, aunts, and uncles who had never really cared much about me. I stopped hating my male cousins when I realized that it was no more their fault for being boys than it was mine for being a girl, but I continued to work and study as if my life depended on it, stacking AP and honors courses onto my academic platter as if I were at a buffet. I wanted to keep my grandmother's love. I needed to prove to the world that I was better than any son my parents might have had. I had to show that I was worthy of other people's love, just like I had proved that I was worthy of my family's.

The French AP guy catches up to me and starts rambling about how overintellectual girls will one day lead to the breakdown of stable nuclear families. Men don't want women more intelligent than themselves; women who are smart and independent have no incentive to get married; the human race will die out because no one will have any more children. Blah blah blah. I resist the urge to sock him in the nose and keep on walking. The only reason he's spouting this bull is that I have one too many X chromosomes.

"Why do you bother?" he repeats for the millionth-and-first time.

I turn my face to glance at him, a little contemptuously. "Because . . ." I trail off and shrug my shoulders lightly.

Because I want to be loved.

— Lisa Wang

Free Willy

On the utterly glacial mornings of the winter months, I always reserve three minutes for myself to stand naked in front of the full-length mirror in our hallway and make faces with my stomach flab. Sometimes I'll pull the base of my cellulite toward my chest and stretch my navel with my fingertips so that my tummy looks a tad surprised, but relatively happy. Sometimes I'll squish together the fat from the left and the fat from the right with my palms so that my belly resembles a constipated pug . . . and sometimes I'll just drum on the sides of my paunch and pretend that a sailboat is crossing my midriff on a fuzzy sea of waving flesh.

It is then that I realize that I am, possibly, a touch strange.

Yes, it is normal to rise in the morning and pour two packets of instant oatmeal into a microwave-safe bowl and prepare breakfast in minutes flat. It is normal to stretch out in one's pajamas and eat the nuked product with a teaspoon, yielding smaller bites and relatively more time to savor the meal. It is normal to allow your dog to lick the bowl.

It is not normal, after consuming the food, to pray that the ingested material will make you pleasingly plump. It is not normal to fantasize about the day when the mirror will reflect a more expansive ocean of portly derma, with even more gargantuan, towering waves that will surely cause sailboats to rock and sailors to hurl and giant squids to surface. It is not normal to *want* to be zaftig — to seek out the glut . . . to take such solace in the Quaker's calories.

But I do.

When I'm stressed, I eat. When I feel pressured, I eat. When

I feel stressed about eating when I'm pressured, I eat. It's quite the routine, and I love it.

To understand, as a teenager, that reality provides little, if any, control over one's own destiny is absolutely horrid. I, personally, can't deal with it. When thinking of myself as helpless I knit my brow and press my index finger to my bottom lip and squirm in my seat and whimper and snivel and moan and hope that *someone* finds it endearing because, Christ, via any other perception, I am pathetic.

I ask myself how it is possible to be powerless when I am so darn haughty and so darn youthful and so darn invincible . . . but then I remember that I'm not invincible, and that I will someday die and that there is, indeed, the possibility that no one will even love me enough to burn my carcass and throw it somewhere. That's depressing, and that's when oatmeal is my best, best bud.

Of course, I'm sure that dealing with stress in such a manner isn't healthy. Oprah Winfrey says it isn't healthy. Oprah says that food is not love and that it is not a security blanket and that it will never ever fill the void that my stress, my pressure, is a result of.

Well, fuck Oprah.

I'm not sure if anyone has ever noticed, but Oprah Winfrey has a massive tush. She's lovely, don't get me wrong, but her fanny is quite large, and I doubt that I should be taking advice from someone with such a giant rump . . . unless, that is, she is fully aware of how stunning and how necessary that rump is.

I think that eating when stressed is a literal defense mechanism. I feel that, someday, all of my fat will dribble away and beneath I will find a layer of titanium armor. I think that I will walk on all fours and live as a rhinoceros, impervious to all outside elements.

I will be thick-skinned. I will not care about the surging rains or the blistering heat or the little white birds that ride on my back. Nothing will hurt me and I will be a tank. School and boys and pimples and cash and George W. Bush cannot stand up to the rhino — and knowing I can squash them all will make my fears dissolve, and I will be as happy as I am when consuming oatmeal.

I want to be as big as a house. I want all of my problems to be tossed into some trash compactor and I want the resulting cube of rubbish to be placed on a scale, on a dish opposite my own, and I want the whole world to see that I am heftier than all of the obstacles of a teenage girl. I want to be the leviathan and I want to be feared and I want kismet to run for the hills when it sees me waddling near. Perhaps, then, no one will contest my modest desire to live forever and I can chisel away at my own eternity in peace.

And so I create balance (or, at least, counterbalance in my favor) with the cunning use of funnel cake . . . or Brie . . . or noodle kugel . . . or a handful of Manischewitz macaroons.

I am aware of the sacrifice. I know, in the end, that there is the chance that I'll have to choose between dates (the fruit) and dates (the men in ironed pants who bring you flowers and compliment you on your hair and take you to a movie and tell you that they're having a grand time and that they want to see you again next Tuesday if you're free or next Friday if you aren't). I am willing to take that chance . . . because men never bring you chocolates anymore and Tuesdays and Fridays are lasagna nights at the local ristorante and movie theater concession stands never sell oatmeal, anyway.

I've never been severely picky and I've never really wanted anything more than the feeling of being sated, of being full. I can only be guaranteed that feeling by a waiter or a grocer or a grandmother, and so I take stock in the stock that they produce . . . and nothing else.

Is it sad? Perhaps. Is it disgusting? It can be. Is it anomalous? You bet your bippy!

I see the most celestial things in fat. I see Buddha. I see the sacred cow. I see the tottering orb that is Earth. I do not see burden or frustration, though; I refuse to see such things.

I have been swallowed whole by the mass, you see. I have surrendered my anxiety to it and, in return, it has granted me voluptuous curves and sweet dimples and a mesmerizing jiggle to my jogging physique.

And I am thankful. And I am free.

Eat your heart out, Jenny Craig.

— Rebecca Bauman

Killers

It's eleven-thirty after the eighth-grade dance on Friday night. The new girl, Carly, stands outside on the blacktop, her white finger on a pearl lighter and a menthol Slim, the ones that come two-fifty a pack and don't last. She needs her own host of angels to hold up that Slim and keep the smoke coming.

She's all white and makes me think of ghosts. The Russian one we read in English — Anna somebody. Karenina. I line up Anna's ghost behind Carly and she's perfect. The Anna ghost wrings her hands, her lips around an O as she waits for a train to hit her.

I don't *like* Carly. I'm not one for friends and I hate girls. I spy on Connie and Jo and Tiffany in the locker room talking cars and their boyfriends' condom sizes, though the only condom they ever saw was the one in Sex Ed and I know it. When the guys talk like that they don't mean it, they don't say it unless someone's listening. Girls must think everyone's listening.

Tiffany comes out in her purple halter top and pleather pants. No boobs on her yet so the top stays up. She saunters over, thinks she's going to try this girl out. See where she fits.

"Hey, Carly, give me a puff." She reaches for it but Carly shakes her head, no-no, you can't. "C'*mon*."

"Can it." I watch Tiffany and her little groupies giggling. It's only me talking, yeah, I'm a harmless bitch to them. Right now I'm not angry.

"I just wanted a puff, *lesbian*." They *ooh* when Tiffany says it.

"Tiff, when're you having Ryan's baby?"

Her little plucked eyebrows snap down. More *oohs* from the peanut gallery. "Don't *talk* to me about my *personal* life, OK?"

Carly's being quiet this whole time. She knows they won't hurt me so she's next in line. An easy target.

"Here." Carly takes out the Slim and hands it to Tiffany. She wants a girl to be her friend. I'll be her friend then. To keep her out of their way.

Tiffany takes these little I'm-so-sexy wheezes and gives the Slim back. "That is *so* gross."

"You didn't ask." I start walking and my earrings jangle. My boots have this *thud* to let lower life-forms know I'm coming. Carly drops the Slim.

"Oh, do you fight?" Connie squeaks in the back and wishes she didn't. Tiffany's mascara runs down her face in globs. She's sweating from the dance.

"What's wrong, Tiff? You're sweating like a prostitute." We stare at each other. I'm no harmless bitch now. Carly waits for us to sort out.

"Crack whore," Tiffany sniffs. She stomps off with the groupies chattering behind her for comfort.

I take Carly's lighter and hold it while she taps out another Slim. I light it for her.

It doesn't take long for Carly to start following me everywhere. We sit on the picnic table and watch the boys play tackle football after lunch. Tiffany and her entourage take up the middle of the field, talking and primping their overbleached hairdos. The math teacher stalks the edge of the field with her whistle.

Carly taps me. "Hi."

I look over. Something's bugging her. "Carly?"

"Hmm?"

"What's up?"

"Nothing." She tosses the pearl lighter from hand to hand. "Why'd you talk to me?"

"You mean on Friday?"

"Yeah."

I think for a second. "Tiffany's such a bitch."

"Oh." Carly squints at the boys on the field. Connie practically leaps in front of the football, but the boys are too quick and go around her.

One of them, Angus, walks off the field. He peels off his sweatshirt to reveal a plain black T-shirt, soaked through.

"Talk to *him*," I tell Carly. "The boys call him Fencepost." Carly nods, puts the lighter back in her pocket. "He sticks up for me."

Angus comes over. He's built like a five-foot-three fence post all right, but not skinny. Just tough. He sits down on the grass in front of me. "Hark, it's good to see you."

"What's up, Angus?"

He shrugs. "I can't do this shit. I hate football."

I slide off the picnic table and plop down next to him. "That's fine. You're not built for it."

Carly inches down real slow and sits on my side away from him. Like she's checking a bear out. Run or stay.

Angus brushes spiky black hair out of his eyes and looks at her. "Are you the new girl?"

"Mm-hm." Her head bobs up and down.

I cut in. "That's Carly."

Angus pokes me. "Nice to see you, Carly." He stands up. "Listen, I'm going." He wipes the dirt off his pants, points at Carly then me. "My house, Saturday. Nine-thirty."

I hold my hand up. He slaps it. "I know where it is," I say. "We'll be there."

I thump the door with my free hand. I've got a bag of Doritos and some Vernors.

"Is this OK?" Carly pokes me in the ribs.

"It means he likes you. We do this all the time."

She shrugs.

Angus opens the door and waves us in. "My dad's got a date tonight. Come in."

I drop the snacks on the table and take a good look around. It looks like it always does. The orange carpet is almost worn away but it's clean. His dad's Brut is hanging stiff in the air. I sneeze.

"Nice house," Carly says.

"Thanks. The downstairs is the best part." Angus grabs the snacks and opens the door to the basement. I flip on the light.

In the basement his dad has their old big-screen TV. Carly looks at it with her mouth open.

Angus laughs. "When my parents split up, my dad got me and the TV. My mom got the rest." I stand on a chair next to the cupboard and flip through his movies. Angus has it all like a video store, alphabetical order. I push out *Psycho*.

"I like that one," Carly says, looking up at me and taking the movie. Angus pops the Doritos bag open and gets some cherry schnapps out of the wine cabinet in the wall. He pours half a shot in a glass of Vernors and holds it out. I shake my head.

"Can't, Angus. I quit last week."

"Did your allergy medicine act up again?"

"Yeah. I can't see straight when I drink."

"Suit yourself. Carly?"

She takes the glass and sips it. She pulls a face and sets it down on the coffee table. We pop in the movie and squeeze in on the couch.

"Watch out for springs," Angus says. We settle in as the movie begins. We're all smiling, even through the shower scene. Angus is sitting in the middle and we both end up hugging him when Tony Perkins comes in with the knife.

On Monday Carly checks her locker and it's got a photo taped in it. I swear she locked it but Tiffany probably got her combination.

The photo's of me from last year and it's a shitty one. It says DIE FREAK in pink gel pen.

"What a giveaway," I say. "Good job, girls."

Carly stares at her locker like it's got a rabid dog in it. I reach over and tear the picture off.

"Carly, they do that a lot. I got one that said 'dyke bitch' last year. You get used to it." She still won't look at me. I can hear Connie squealing down the hall as they watch us.

Carly picks up her books and grabs my arm. "C'mon," she says. "We'll miss biology."

I sit by Angus in art class and work on the potter's wheel. My smock's all full of clay but I've got the curve just right on a jug. Maybe for my mom this Christmas, if it doesn't crack.

Angus is cutting something out with the meanest-looking

scissors I've ever seen. He's going so fast the paper's all over. I can't tell what he's making.

"Hark?" He puts down the scissors. "Did Carly find that note?"

"What do you think?" I widen the lip on my jug.

"She wouldn't talk to me." Angus starts cutting again. "I saw them making it after school last week. I thought it was for you."

I shake my head. The clay's getting dry. "I did, too, when I saw it. Just says 'die freak' in pink pen on my picture."

Angus brushes paper off his shirt. "I wish they'd leave her alone. She takes it hard."

I'm gritting my teeth while I squeeze the clay. I know this jug will work, I know it's good — but my thumb goes through the side.

I kick the off switch. "Fuck!"

Angus looks down at the lump of clay. I sit there thinking and he unfolds his paper. It's a perfect spiderweb pattern. "It just needs a fly stuck in the middle," he says.

I check the front of Carly's locker every day, but I don't know her combination so there's always something new inside. The classic YOU'RE A LESBIAN and GO FUCK YOURSELF notes come rolling in.

Then they corner us by the picnic table to see if the notes are working yet. Angus gives up football after lunch and hangs out with us, so he's there when they come strutting up on Friday.

This time Jo gets a shot at being ringleader. "Hey, smoker girl."

Carly won't look at her. I try to stand up but Angus tugs me down.

Jo tries again. "I said, *talk* to me." Jo's the fake hip-hopper with big hoop earrings and silver-purple lipstick. She thinks she's Lil' Kim. I just think she's a skank-fest.

She hooks her thumb in her low-rise glitter jeans and leans into Carly's face. "You smell like shit. You know that?" Little gasps from the audience in the back.

Angus gives Jo a stare that would kill Charles Manson. Connie stops laughing, squeaks, and tugs on Jo's arm. "Let's go. C'mon."

Jo shrugs her off. "Are you deaf, dirtbag?" she shouts in Carly's face. No answer, but Carly's hands shake as the girls start laughing again. Jo sashays off, with her girls chirping admiration.

Carly's still shaking. She gets up slow and goes inside for the bathroom. I follow her and Angus keeps a lookout.

In the girls' bathroom I find her in a pink stall, smoking another Slim.

"The janitor'll catch you, Carly. C'mon out." I stand in front of her. She shakes her head and puffs harder. "God dammit! Jo can't kill you."

She blinks like she's going to cry. "They all can."

"*Those* girls? I'll kick their asses if that's what you want."

"No." She reaches for the stall door. "Leave me alone."

I snap the Slim out of her hand and toss it in the trash. "Get up and come talk to me!"

"I'm talking."

"Not like that. It's their problem we're weird, not ours. Understand?"

She shakes her head. "It happened last time, too."

"Your last school?"

She nods. "They hate me."

"Oh, Christ —" I lean on the stall. "We're in this, too, OK? Me. You. Angus."

Carly leans forward until I can't see her face for her dark red-streaked hair. It's straight and greasy. I step out of the stall. "Come out when you're ready," I say. She stays quiet.

The next day she won't speak to me. When I go to talk to her, that Anna ghost is standing there behind Carly, shaking her head.

Carly brings a book to school and stuffs her nose in it. She lets the notes collect on her locker door like favorite pictures of old friends. Angus asks her to come over for another movie but she says no. She never talks to us again.

When I find a picture in my locker on Thursday, I don't just toss it. I study the photo — an Internet printout of a girl all gagged up with black tape. She has long straight hair like Carly's and her eyes are blacked out with marker.

On Saturday night my parents are out at a movie. I get a brick and a bucket of red paint and walk to Connie's house at midnight. They're having a sleepover, and the girls are giggling inside, with Britney Spears on full blast. I can see Connie in sky-blue pajamas, probably telling some grade-school joke about sex. They're munching microwave popcorn straight out of the bag.

I dip the brick in the bucket and hurl it at the bedroom window. They start screaming over the Britney Spears music.

"Ohmigod! OH MY GOD!"

"WHAT THE FUCK!"

Tiffany runs to the window in red pajamas, pink curlers rattling. She looks at me, her mouth open in the same *O* as Carly's.

I look down at my arms full of red paint. As I run back to my house I think of how many times I've been called a fucking bitch. I wish I'd spat at Jo when she leaned in Carly's face and killed her.

— Alice Rose Lott

a boy with glasses

there is a picture in my locker of me
wearing eyeglasses, and sometimes people

walk by and say that i look good in those
frames, and i always have to tell them that

they aren't mine, but belong to a boy
i met one summer, a Jewish boy with

glasses like those, who wrote poetry and
listened to rap music, and i tell them

how i still talk to him sometimes, and
how he sends me self-portraits with

longer hair, and told me once about
how he found a toilet in a park and scribbled

verse all over its porcelain curves until he
flung it over a cliff. and sometimes we

talk about racism versus anti-Semitism
and about how he prefers black girls to white ones,

curvature to non, and sometimes we
talk about lyricism, and loss, and

writing, and hip-hop, and about how
hard it is to live the way we want to now;

and about why he doesn't have a loved one;
and about how he'll never make

it as a beatnik because creativity is suicide;
and about how he'll never survive dependence,

or adolescence, or his future, and so forth
until it comes to the point where i am forced

to threaten to cut him open and show
his hemorrhaged but happy heart harder times.

— Branden Jacobs-Jenkins

The Relationship Between Lovers and Words

"Times like these. Someone is writing and we are only words."
— Xai

I. Bergamot
a small tree
there you were beneath it and lifting one arm up,
throwing one arm back,
in a Venetian garden (I think;
the details are unclear now, muted nouns)
and reaching for it, stretching and reaching,
while the strangest nakedness bathed your body, softened by sunlight.
I thought:
if only I could paint you as you are
in my deepest of dreams,
with sour citrus fruits.

II. Astrolabes
a medieval invention
plotted the course of our stars today; jokingly,
we listen to the fortune teller who says
"You were alchemists in a life past,
but I do not know if you were lovers
or enemies"
as she plotted the course of your hand,

the lines drawn zodiacally
to determine the altitude of the sun.

III. Chrysoprase
an apple-green chalcedony
lay there imagined in the hollow of your neck
where collarbone met collarbone,
the smooth white and the gemstone like a beetle
burrowing against you;
like Egypt, your beloved country,
and the distance between us desert after desert,
and the touch of your skin a cool Nile against my skin,
and the flash of your heart like a buried beetle
used as a gemstone.

IV. Marjoram
aromatic plants
each a reminder that I should know how to smell you
how to trace your scent
with my lips, how to touch it
with my breath,
how to spread you against me
like a delicacy,
or let you grow without my help,
in a garden I am not the first to imagine
with small bruise-white flowers.

V. Windjammer

a
time ago, a long time ago,
(for you believe in past lives and inherited lovers,
karmic intervention as opposed to divine intervention,
that I have slept with you before, many times
and will sleep with you again, many times
though we may not sleep with each other
this time around)
we sailed together, you explain, beneath the storm-swirled sky
from Italy to somewhere
(the somewhere did not count;
we drowned the third day)
on a
large sailing ship.

VI. Windlass

a machine for
every task and every purpose: this is our place,
to design, to machinate,
to mechanize appropriate mechanisms.
And so you too have allowed yourself to be useful,
you have designed this oblique cylinder
and have raised my heart bastioned upon it like
raising weights.

VII. Marten

a mammal related to the weasel
I may not be, but still you hunt me,
and each day wear a new piece of me around your neck
with a slender body, bushy tail, soft fur.

VIII. Damascene

metalwork
in these ancient days:
bowed over books I, transcribing with crying quill,
and you, in the fire of the forges,
dirt upon your cheeks and heat upon your hands.
Somehow despite this I have come to understand
that you were building me then, and I did not know
how intricate the detail,
decorated with patterns of curling inlay.

IX. Estuary

where the sea
is lapping, lapping, lapping,
and you and I are simply napping
my head upon your easy breast,
a storm is brewing in the West.
And one of us is singing, singing
to the water, bringing, bringing,
elsewhere the bells are ringing, ringing
the salty water stinging, stinging.
(What comes of this? My lover queried;

time beneath the ocean buried.)
And here our twenty fingers quiver —
twilight comes and
meets the river.

X. Garret

a room
hid us. We were only children.
We were only dirty-faced children.
We were only uninspiring children.
Still, we gathered old coal like buried treasure
and painted our faces black and blacker,
pretended we were chimney sweeps
and with an old broomstick I felt in love with you
though I forgot not to die three months later
of a cold caught
on the top floor of the house, typically under a pitched roof.

XI. Haymow

a pile of hay
a clear, cool day — I bring you your dinner,
you eat it slow. Here, we romp and rut
and leave smelling like animals
raised
in a barn.

XII. Belvederes

pavilions or towers on top of a building
where we looked out at the world spread all-ways around us
here there was mist,
there, a rising sunlight and a red sky,
to the left of us the stables,
while to the right of us the hills rolled on and on
like a graveyard. (If you followed them long enough,
you would come to the graveyard.)
It is not a clear day, but we can see forever up here,
commanding a wide view.

XIII. Sirocco

a hot
day and an unlucky number. What words you have picked!
you say;
and what fruits you pick as you say it.
Would that we were better with peaches;
still, we are devouring figs.
Such is the landscape. Such is our current predicament.
Almonds, dates, and oil lamps.
(I will dance for you, I promise,
I will dance for you and when the last veil falls
I will be nothing more than one noun,
your noun.
Such is the fate of man.
Such is the fate of a devoted lover.)

It begins to blow over us all,
this fate,
this
humid southerly wind.

— Hannah Jones

Shah Noor

Aunty sat in a white plastic lawn chair behind the counter with her head bent toward her lap. Strands of loose hair in a variety of colors — gray, white, henna red, and black — all hung from her head. Age had not only affected her hair color, but also its quantity. Parts of her curved back went uncovered, revealing a plain black pashmina shawl that wrapped her body. Nobody would realize that there was another human being in the store, next to Uncle behind the counter. Her chair had a fixed position — beside the right wall, behind the blue and white CHICKEN DUM BIRIYANI, RS. 55 sign that sat atop the marble-top counter. Aunty always sat there silently, her head facing her lap, whether there was a throng of customers inside the store or only the humid monsoon wind blowing in from the open back door.

Uncle went about his work, restocking the trays in the display case under the counter with freshly fried chicken *farcha* and rearranging the *sheekh kebabs* so they formed a pyramid. He moved skillfully around the room from the stove in the back to the counter up front, carefully turning around table corners and bending down to reach the cabinets — all without ever saying "excuse me" to his wife or asking her to shift her position. As *shami kebabs* sizzled and cracked in a pot of oil, Aunty remained in her usual position, with her head down and her eyes focused on the string of beads that her frail hand clutched. Her long fingers carefully pulled one bead after another along the black string as her thin lips parted slightly to emit a prayer. As one bead fell upon another, a muffled *tk* filled the air, joining the chorus of noise produced by Uncle's shoes rubbing against the marble-tiled floor and the hissing kebabs. Aunty

175

remained seated, oblivious to her husband's bustle, unaffected by the beeping of the microwave or the heat coming from the stove, the monsoon breezes, and the black Kashmiri wool.

The stores in Pune cantonment opened at eleven and then closed at one. In those two afternoon hours, Uncle had to sell as many of his Mughal delights as he could. At half past noon, hordes of young journalists from the neighboring *Indian Express* office in Aurora Towers began flowing into his store. All those who had forgotten to pack lunch, or those for whom Mummy didn't have time to prepare chapati, or others who lived on their own and didn't know how to cook anything except rice and lentils turned to Uncle for a meal. Their presence transformed the quiet store into a makeshift hangout, where the sizzle of the fry pan became muffled by *Arre* and *yaar* — the *hey* and *yo* of India.

"Hello, Uncle," called out a chirpy voice.

"Hello, my dear," said Uncle, turning around to see dark red lipstick-smothered lips, the source of the voice.

"Uncle, I would like two coffees. Parcel, please," she asked sweetly while adjusting the *odni* of her *salwar-kameez*.

"Yes, please, Miss." Uncle turned his back once again and walked over to the automatic Nescafé coffee machine. "Anything else, please, Miss?" he asked. The girl shook her head, and Uncle once again turned his attention to the coffee machine.

With his short, chubby finger he pressed the button. The black spout emitted burning-hot coffee into a flimsy plastic cup, which Uncle then covered with a small square of aluminum foil that fit across the cup's opening perfectly. *Minimize the costs and maximize the profits.*

Once the girl had approved of her *odoni*'s position, she reached into her purse and pulled out a five-rupee coin. She placed it on the counter, and Uncle quickly deposited it into a box. He looked up at her with the usual broad grin on his face and she dove into her purse once again.

"Uncle, I don't have five rupees more for the other coffee. I only have a hundred note. Do you have change?"

Uncle reluctantly maintained the smile upon his face. He hated having to break notes and give change. But most of all he hated promises for future payment. "No, sorry, my dear. I do not," he answered sweetly, tilting his head a bit to the side and slightly pouting his mouth.

"*Phir me kal deungi*, Uncle. Tomorrow, I promise."

For a moment Aunty left her solemn world of prayer and turned her eyes to her husband, who stood there with that artificial smile spread across his face. She glared at him, and he felt the heat of her stare and turned his head to look directly into her two raven-black beady eyes filled with anger and shame. *Do something!* her eyes called out to their companion pair. *Don't let yourself be taken advantage of by these children who never pay the correct amount!*

But Uncle ignored the silent orders of his wife. "All right, my dear, you come tomorrow," he said to the young girl, conceding to the wishes of his customer. Aunty quickly turned her head down, avoiding her husband's gray cowardly eyes.

"Oh, thank you, Uncle. Tomorrow. Five rupees. Without fail," the girl replied. Just as she was leaving the store, she stopped for a moment in front of the full-length mirror right beside the entrance.

177

Once again she adjusted her *odni*, then stepped out, carrying the two hot coffees in her hands.

One after another, Uncle's other lunchtime friends, all his dears and sons, waltzed into the store, asking for coffee, kebabs, and burgers — the last an addition to the menu to satisfy the cravings of this cosmopolitan crowd.

"Hello, Uncle. Hello, Aunty," called out a kurta-clad boy.

The usual friendly, wide grin spread across Uncle's face, revealing pearly white teeth in the midst of a gray, stubby beard. Having been addressed directly for the first time, Aunty looked up and paused her prayer, disrupting the rhythm of the beads.

"*Kya haal hai*, Aunty? Taking care of yourself?" Aunty's thin lips moved out a quarter of an inch, a gesture that told the young boy she was fine. Uncle kept the same broad smile upon his face.

"How are you, my son?" asked Uncle. Aunty returned to her position, continuing with her prayers and holding beads alternately in her hands.

"Oh, just fine, thank you, Uncle."

"What would you like, please?"

The journalist turned his head down to the glass display case, eyeing the orange-colored Tandoori *paneer* and the long cylindrical *sheekh kebabs* that sat there, neglected by journalists searching for a quick, simple, stomach-filling meal. After minutes of contemplating *shami*, *sheekh*, or *chapal kebabs*, the young man finally opted for a chicken burger.

"Chicken burger parcel, Uncle." The boy stood in front of the counter with his hands in his jeans pockets, slowly rocking on his heels.

"Yes, please. One minute, please." Uncle turned around, making his way to the stove where he had already kept a chicken burger for heating, knowing that one of his customers would want an American-style lunch. As he flipped the burger over, the steam from the sizzling patty fogged his glasses. Uncle removed them and rubbed the corner of his cotton handkerchief across the thick, foggy bifocal lenses. While holding his glasses up to the tube light for inspection, Uncle's eyes wandered to the handwritten motto that hung on the wall before him:

CUSTOMER SERVICE ENDS WHEN THE CUSTOMER SAYS NO

Uncle took these words to heart. The faded pink writing was the principle he lived by, meaning more to him than all the teachings of the holy men Salim Chisti and Mullah Salauddin Massod, whose photos hung high up on the wall behind his wife's chair. To make sure that he would never hear a customer say no, he inserted *please* into almost all of his sentences, and always had that broad, clownish grin spread across his face.

When the patty had turned golden brown on both sides, Uncle lifted it off the frying pan and placed it into a bun already dressed with a tomato slice. Realizing that his order was ready, the young man plunged his hands deeper into his pockets and pulled out a fifty-rupee note. Uncle handed the man a brown bag containing his meal and carefully picked up the note from the counter. He held the note at its ends and stared at Gandhi in the watermark. Looking into Gandhi's gentle eyes hidden behind circular lenses was no comfort to Uncle, whose mind was haunted by the memory of his wife's black eyes. The thought of her piercing stare frightened him into summoning the courage to ask the boy for the exact amount — twenty-two rupees.

However, nothing came out of his mouth. Fearing that his customer would say no held back the anger that burned within him. Instead a broad smile spread across his face as he opened the metal box and pulled out three ten-rupee notes. The red-lipstick girl owed him five rupees and this *kurta* boy owed him two. There was still another hour for business, another hour for promises of future payment, which at times were made and at times forgotten.

He could feel his wife's venomous glare eating through his flesh, making its way through his cowardly innards as he placed one ten-rupee note in the young journalist's hand. His wife, with her wild, multicolored hair flying up and down, danced in his mind, twirling the black Kashmiri shawl around her. "Shah Noor," she called out menacingly. "King of Light is an unworthy name for one who is the slave of cowardice."

Indeed, she was right. He was nothing more than the slave of cowardice, adjusting himself to the caprices of his customers and refusing to assert himself. Feeling miserable, upset, and hollow, he maintained the broad grin on his face and handed back the second ten-rupee note. *Slave of cowardice* rang through his mind, devouring whatever self-worth was left within his slight body. Just as the slave of cowardice extended his hand to give the young man the final ten-rupee note, Shah Noor pulled back his hand.

"Why don't you ever come here with the proper amount ready?" Shah Noor asked suddenly, his voice filled with frustration. "You know my prices, you always order chicken burgers and coffees, but are ready to pay for them with thousand-rupee notes!"

There was silence. The wind stopped at the doorway and the beads froze in their positions. Aunty lifted her head. The journalist was startled. Uncle had a reputation for being one of the sweetest men, always friendly, cheerful, and understanding, especially when it came to pecuniary matters. But that Uncle no longer stood in front of him.

"What do you think this is?" Shah Noor continued with his impassioned tirade. "The Mughal Emperor's canteen? How do you walk the streets without two rupees' change in your hands? I can't understand such logic!"

Shocked, the young man once again searched his pocket and removed a shiny two-rupee coin. "Here, sir. I thought I didn't have any change. I'm sorry about that," he said, his voice trembling slightly. "I think that's all I owe you."

"Yes. That's all," confirmed Shah Noor. Once the account had been settled, the young man took the parcel and scampered out of the store like a dog that had been threatened with a stone.

Suddenly Aunty removed herself from her plastic chair and walked over to the counter. She picked up the two-rupee coin and placed it in the palm of her hand. Lying there, the brand-new, fresh-from-the-mint coin shimmered and glowed like the full moon. "Shah Noor," she said proudly, extending her hand out to her husband, "*Yeh hai apkar*; this belongs to you."

Shah Noor took his coin from his wife's hand and placed it in his metal box.

— Vanashree Samant

181

The Marriage Proposal

His shape reminds her mostly
of a lump of gingerroot.
He unfolds from the car's
hood where he waited for her
to finish work. She suspects that
of the few men who have kissed her
he will be the last. Pause. Breathe. *Yes.*

This decision will fling her
into a life where the burners
of her stove will melt the good
soup ladle. The smoke from his
cigars will burn the backs of her
eyes — dry enough to choke.
Food will not fill her; words will be scarce
her skirts will fade and fall out of fashion.

Only dreams like sweet juice
sliding down her throat,
of red love tasting sugary-lemon
of flamenco with rocking hips
stamping heels and a red dress
of cascading ruffles like feathers
of flowers as big as her face
so perfect they must be poisoned.

— Freya Gibbon

thursday night soliloquies

i.

late in the day, lights go on across the city
as people raise electric faces to the sky.
your shadow is draped loose and black across the floor,
stunned; too sleepy to fly away.

ii.

i hold the phone to me like a face
imagining that my breath
goes straight to your lips

iii.

my hands leave white prints on the window.
i am leaning forward, looking for your face
though every moment clouds the clear glass
                                   more.

iv.

you pronounce love in syllables of coffee.
i am drinking and praying never to reach the bottom
of this cup.

— Kristin Ferebee

Seven Spots

Everything is going just fine until Mae starts decorating her house with insects. It begins with the *Insect Lover's Encyclopedia* the other librarians give her after her fifth year of working at the Liberty, Georgia, branch. In its preface, the encyclopedia for insect lovers explains that it is actually an encyclopedia for *arthropod* lovers because besides being about insects, it also includes myriapods (anything with more than eight legs) and arachnids. Mae likes myriapods all right, as far as she can tell, but she is certain that she doesn't love arachnids. It isn't so much the ticks and spiders that bother her. It's the scorpions, even though she has only seen one, when she was nine years old and hiking with her Girl Scouts troop. (She remembers a small, redheaded girl pointing into the dirt, squealing, "Look! Look!" Mae backed away from the other girls, all of them crowding around the first. The leader noticed Mae and pulled her over, telling her that she wouldn't get the Exploration badge if she didn't at least look.)

Insects of the six-legged variety, however, have Mae from the beginning. The first item, the birth of her museum, is a single ladybug she finds in the freshly cut grass by the mailbox. Mae has never cut the grass, so it is the first thing her boyfriend, Lou, owner of the white Lawns by Lou truck parked in her front yard every day now, does for her when he moves in. "Now you can actually see the house!" he proclaims after he turns off the lawn mower. Lou sweeps his arm out over the yard, toward the small brick house where Mae has always lived. He grins, and the sun shines on his premature bald spot, on his forehead, on his wide nose, on his chin. Lou is gleaming, Mae realizes, with delight. She would hug him for it, were it not for that single red ladybug she spies poised on an arched blade of grass. Yes, it is this ladybug that causes Mae to open the *Insect Lover's Encyclopedia* to page seventy-three, where a sentence in the lower left-hand corner of the page triumphantly renames that common creature the *Coccinella septempunctata*. The seven-spot ladybird.

Of course, Mae comes to like the sound of the classification names for every insect, but the seven-spot ladybird's is forever her favorite. *Coccinella septempunctata* is what she declares into the telephone, a greeting, when she calls her parents, who have just moved seventy-three miles away and into Florida. It is what Mae replaces the words of several show tunes with when she washes dishes, singing it out over porcelain and suds. It is even what she whispers into the left ear of Lou, a tribute to their seven months together (seven spots!), while she is falling asleep against the earthy smell of him. The truth is, even when Mae does not know what to say, it is just what she says: *Coccinella septempunctata*.

By the time Mae has a total of nineteen seven-spot ladybirds, she is coming straight home from the library every day, then collecting all the six-legged creatures she can find. Lou drives up after work to see her standing on the front porch, her arms wrapped around the huge pickle jar she keeps them in until she can organize them. Lou is already tired of the bugs. "It's a messy hobby," he tells her at dinner as he carefully watches the jar that has been placed between the squash casserole and the green beans. He eyes its lid and reads *Diplopoda*.

"See how it's rolled up? That's called conglobation," Mae says, pointing through the glass at one of the seven total millipedes, one that is curled into a ball. Lou cranes his neck a little, just enough to see. "Anyway, it's not that messy. I organize them." Which is true, she does organize them. By now she has a place in the house for every insect she has ever found. The praying mantis always goes in the bathroom, in the single tub with the claw feet, in a duct-taped and hole-punched shoe box labeled *Coccinellidae*. The jars in the small, seldom-used fireplace and on the bookshelves beside it are each marked *Lucanidae* for the two stag beetles, who will wrestle to death if they aren't separated.

The old juice bottles on the kitchen table and in the drawers of the dressers are filled with six (at most recent count) moth caterpillars, only identified as belonging to the large and inclusive *Lepidoptera* family. Two of the original eight have crawled up into cocoons that stick to the side of the glass, so Mae has taken the lids and moved their bottles to the windowsill above her scuppernong vines. It is summertime, so Mae even catches *Lampyridae*, those neon-tipped fireflies she can keep in jars, jars she places in the flower box with her tulips.

On Monday night, when Lou is asleep, Mae opens the drawer of the bedside table where she is keeping three baby-food jars full of black ants. She lifts one to eye level, watches the small bodies scramble over one another, thinking of the strength each contains. She imagines herself collecting ant after ant, drawing them into jar after jar with trails of confectioners' sugar. Then, when there are hundreds or even thousands of them, she will set them free in the house, where they will find her limp body in its sleep. Perhaps they will hoist her above their heads and carry her deep into the earth, into the tunnels beneath the humble red hills in her front yard. Underground, Mae could learn their silent languages, one where things are felt, where these feelings are passed through the air from one outstretched antenna to another.

One morning, later, the flower box falls, spilling the contents of those jars, mostly just dead leaves and dirt. But there are no fireflies, because it is late summer and the thrill of *Lampyridae* is fading, rising beyond Mae with the heat of August. She picks up the jars, and when she goes into the kitchen for breakfast, Lou is there. Lou usually sleeps until nine, she knows, long after she's left for work. "What are you doing?" Mae asks, pouring herself a glass of whole milk. She has never drunk anything but whole milk, which she is proud of and likes to tell people, even ones she's just met. It makes her feel like an interesting *and* healthy person; it seems to her that it's getting harder to find someone who is both. Lou watches her from the kitchen table, where he sits in the bathrobe Mae gave him for Christmas.

"Good morning," Lou says, his rough morning voice breaking the silence, carrying out over the clink of glass in the silverware drawer where Mae was looking for a spoon. Glass jars, Lou knows.

"Caterpillars," Mae says, her voice purring softly, reminding Lou of the time he overheard her on the kitchen phone, telling her mother about him for the first time. *He's Lou*, she had said, holding the mouthpiece of the receiver up to her lips with both hands, letting the other end rest on her shoulder. Then she hung up without saying good-bye and, afterward, stood in front of the sink for a long time.

After she finds a spoon, Mae takes a grapefruit half from the refrigerator and places it on the kitchen table. "Why don't you go back to sleep?" she asks Lou, as if she had only just recognized the man sitting beside her. "Since you're already awake, actually, could you fix the flower box?" With that, she walks out of the kitchen to get ready for work. She is usually grumpy in the mornings.

When she comes home that afternoon, the flower box is gone and there's a new swing on the side of the porch facing west. It is a perfect place for the crickets.

"It's not for crickets, Mae. It's so you have a place to sit when the sun goes down," Lou explains later, while they are having dinner. That's when they get most of their talking in, at dinnertime. Lou is chewing on mashed potatoes, and telling himself that he is a reasonable man. It is important for him to remember that he is a reasonable man because he is about to tell Mae to get rid of all the bugs. He is going to need reasons. He sticks his fork into his mashed potatoes, upright. "Mae!" He says it a little too loudly though, and her spoon clangs against her glass.

"Christ, Lou, I'm sitting right here," she says.

"Mae. Excuse me. Mae. I want to talk about something. It's the insects. I think they're getting to be a little too much. They're showing up in strange places," he says, quickly but firmly. Lou is talking about the bathtub in particular. He had only just discovered the European praying mantis that very morning as he was taking a shower.

"Well. I'm a collector, Lou. What do you expect a collector to do with her collection?" This is a serious question.

"I just think they would be better off outside. That's where bugs belong," Lou answers. He takes another bite of his mashed

188

potatoes. The truth is, he is, number one, afraid of losing Mae and, number two, afraid of having to find somewhere else to live.

"I'll take care of them," Mae says. As she stands, she reaches for Lou's plate.

They get ready for bed earlier than usual. Lou sits by the window smoking his favorite pipe, his only pipe, the very same pipe his father used to smoke. Mae climbs beneath the covers and feels under her pillow for her *Insect Lover's Encyclopedia*. "What if we make a garden? The bugs will stay there," Lou says, lying on his back. He doesn't read as much as Mae does. On page forty-seven is a section about *Formicidae*. Beside a picture of an ant it reads, *Two adult ants may precede a food transfer with mutual antennal tapping, as well as the begging ant gently stroking the cheeks of the donor.*

Mae looks over at Lou's cheeks. She remembers how she noticed them first, how round and pink they are, like a child's. "A garden, Lou? The bugs will eat the plants." Mae licks her index finger and uses it to turn the page. She has always liked to do it that way because it feels old-fashioned. Mae likes things she can call old-fashioned.

"We don't really need the plants. And in a garden, you could also keep some earthworms. Those aren't insects, I know, but they like gardens," which may as well be the end of it because Lou is rambling the way he does when he falls asleep. He begins to snore and rolls over until his back is to Mae. She closes the encyclopedia and puts it on the floor beside her. Of course she isn't tired; her mind is whirring with the possibilities of earthworms. *Earthworms*, she says to herself, an inaudible twist of her lips. Lou is right, they aren't insects. Mae doesn't know their Latin names, but maybe that's the way it should start. *Perhaps the earthworms could be different*, Mae thinks to herself. Earthworms *are* different. They aren't millipedes, with their mechanical acrobatics. They aren't beetles with their intent to kill, life-and-death dependent on Mae's fancies for organization. Earthworms aren't the sluggish moth caterpillars with their promise of, eventually, flight. And never would an earthworm be the blessed ladybird with her seven spots and nomenclature that could very well have been the death of the Latin language — *Coccinella septempunctata*.

When Mae gets home the next day, she decides to start on the earthworms. Actually, the decisions have long been made; they are sliding around in her head as they have been since the earliest hours of the morning. All day at the library, she has been working through the obstacles, which is really only one obstacle: the Lawn by Lou. Lou has been working on the yard for a long time, since the beginning, since the very day that the ladybug became the seven-spotted bird. By now it is spread smooth with thick grass, dotted with small shrubs and bushes, plugged with a sprinkler system and lined, against the street, with hedges. It looks fine, all right, but Mae knows there are bound to be earthworms underneath the well-kempt facade.

Mae begins in the front yard. She is crawling around on her hands and knees, sliding an old paint bucket deep into the damp soil so that when she lifts it again it is full of the earth and her worms. Mae has filled one bucket with the front yard by the time the craters are becoming noticeable. Mae decides to move to the backyard, and when that surface has been exhausted, she tries her neighbors' side yard. By the time she goes inside, she has three buckets full to the top with an indeterminate number of earthworms slipping around in a mixture that is mostly soil plus a little of the red bark mulch Lou just put out beneath the hedges. She didn't mean to pick that up.

Mae is a little unsure about how to care for the earthworms but decides that they will be fine in the buckets. She ends up putting the buckets on the kitchen table, right beside the moth caterpillars, while she starts supper. She is peeling potatoes when she hears Lou's truck pull up in front of the house. She waits by the sink for what seems like a long time, until Lou opens the front door and calls to her. She is expecting him to notice the yard, of course.

"Mae?" he calls, his voice low and steady. Mae turns on the sink in reply, hoping the sound of the water will suffice for her answer, her coordinates. "Mae, I saw the yard. I think this has something to do with your collections" — a poor expression of a worthless observation. He is not yet in the kitchen, but he is close. "We really do need to talk about this." And he almost doesn't, but at the last minute he adds, "I would be happier if we could do something about the bugs." He is in the doorway between the kitchen and the den, but Mae does not turn around to look at him. "I know you hear me," he continues, but then he sees the table, the three buckets piled high with dirt, worms crawling through its mass. He lifts the palm of his hand to his forehead, and Mae is sure that he understands what has happened. Lou looks at her, his eyes widening and his lips parted slightly.

"They're for the garden, Lou. You said, last night, that they could be for the garden," Mae says, then adds, "I'm sorry about the yard." The apology is carefully dropped into the space between them, quickly and efficiently, as if there was no time to waste. Mae moves over to the kitchen table and grabs the pails by their plastic handles. She is picking them up when the phone rings and Lou answers it. Mae listens only until she hears Lou say, "She did *what* to your side yard?" With that, Mae takes off through the house, slower than usual because of the three heavy buckets bouncing around at the end of both of her arms. Lou hangs up the phone and runs after her.

It does not take him long to catch up with her. He wraps his arms around her from behind and lifts her off her feet. She is small, much smaller than he, so he's careful. "That was Mrs. Weber, next door. She says you've ruined her side yard. That is what I mean, exactly." Lou isn't yelling, but he is talking louder than usual. Mae squirms a little in his arms and drops the buckets. She is actually thinking about the end of *Butch Cassidy and the Sundance Kid*, where the two guys end up getting caught. The police tell them to come out with their hands up, but they don't do it. Instead, they run out into the square with their guns and get all shot to pieces. They knew that was going to happen, but they ran out with their guns anyway. Something like that. Mae has always hated the end of that movie.

"Lou, I don't feel so good," she tries to say, but she is having trouble talking with Lou squeezing her. "Please put me down," she manages to ask, and Lou obeys her. He sets her on her feet but does not let go of her arms.

"Just let some of them go. Keep one of each or something!" Lou says to her. He is excited about having Mrs. Weber on his side. Mae isn't sure what to do, really. She leans her forehead in so that it rests on the breast pocket of Lou's work shirt. Lou lets go of her hands and hugs her. "Only some of them," he says again, and he isn't shouting this time. Now she is thinking that she doesn't care about bugs so much. They're fine, she tells herself, but she could be just as happy collecting other things. Bottle caps, for example, or ink pens. "*Coccinella septempunctata,*" she whispers, though Lou doesn't hear.

— Anna Lister

Where the Floor Meets the Ceiling:
words that don't exist but should

antidextrous (an' ti dek' strus) *adj.* easily getting your left and right mixed up, especially in a crucial moment like giving or following important directions

armnesia (arm nee' zhu) *n.* when you raise your arm in class and forget what you were going to say once you're called on

biofickle (bi' o fik ul) *adj.* when you get hot with your coat on so you take it off, but then you get cold with it off

converse-deprevity (con' vurse de prev' it ee) *n.* when you have something you really want to add to the conversation and then someone changes the subject

curft (kerft') *n.* a gift that is a curse; e.g., you're really smart so you end up doing your best bud's homework every night

disposichairy (dis paws' ich ary) *adj.* to describe those chairs that you simply cannot find the "just right" sitting position in

equilibriats (ee kwi li' bree atz) *n.* those who play mind games on their little sibling(s) (if you ever meet a poor, deranged little child, you now know that she/he has an equilibriat for an older sibling)

found and lost disorder (fownd and lawst dis or' der) *n.* constantly tripping over something you don't need or want around but can't find when you start looking for it

hydrostasis (hi dro stay' sis) *n.* always putting your face too close to the water fountainhead so that the water goes in your eyes and nose

lockinterextrication (lok' in ter ex tri kay' shun) *n.* when you shut and lock your locker (other doors apply, too) and then find that you either have something you forgot to get out or something you forgot to put inside

mind hazing (mind hay' zing) *v.* doing better on tests that you don't study for

neurotics (nu rot' iks) *n.* the feeling that you're still wearing a hat even hours after you've taken it off

phaging pit (fay' jing pit') *n.* the place where all the food that guys eat goes, allowing them to eat forever and still be hungry

premonitters (pre moan itt' urs) *n.* the feeling that you've forgotten something but you don't know what

roomtide (rume' tide) *n.* that force that pulls you into your bedroom once you get to the top of the stairs, making you momentarily forget where you were headed in the first place

snudge (snuj) *n.* that little strip of dirt you end up sweeping under the rug because it just won't sweep into the dustpan

spinal blindspot (spine' ul blind' spot) *n.* that one place on your back that always itches and is impossible to reach

squibbler (skwi' blur) *n.* a person who asks questions for the pure sake of asking questions, especially ones with no answers or ones that make the person look dumb without realizing it; e.g., in the middle of a dumb blond joke (DBJ), a squibbler will forget it's a DBJ and ask what color hair the person in the joke has

sqwaffle (skwa' full) *n.* the state of mind where you take in little, unnoticeable details yet focus on nothing

vocabulization-misplacion (vo cab' yew lize a' shun-miss place' shun) *n.* the state where your mind gets boggled and you start mixing up your sentences and then when people look at you funny you forget what you just said; e.g., when you say "my tie is unshoed"

vocality (vo kal' i tee) *n.* to start shouting something to the person next to you in order to be heard in a loud room, not noticing when the noise dies down and your voice rings throughout the building

vu ja de (voo zha day) *n.* when you feel like you've been someplace before but haven't

wibbley (wib' lee) *adj.* when a person never has a preference when you ask them their opinion; oftentimes a very nerve-racking quality

xymphony (zim' fone ee) *n.* a great concert that the neighborhood kids gather for, when you bang on pots with spoons and strum on rubber bands stretched between your fingers and teeth

yaktalker (yak' taw ker) *n.* a person who talks so much that when you're on the phone you have enough time to set the phone down to get a glass of milk and a snack and come back to find them yakking away without ever noticing your absence

zocabulackary search (zoe cab' u lak air' ee) *n.* when you look something up in the dictionary and there are words in the definition that you have to look up

— Sarah Benson

Shit Happens

You know what people say when I tell them I got run over by the same goddamn bus six times? Shit. No shit, I say, bus number twenty-goddamn-seven. It's why I ride the subway now instead of walking. That's a lot of times to get run over by the same goddamn bus, they say. No shit, I say, you're telling me. Three different drivers, too. Well you know what they say, they say. Shit happens. I know they say that, I say. I got run over by the same bus six times. What the hell does *shit happens* mean? I know shit happens. Look at me. I'm shit. I'm happened. What the hell do I mean? Give me all your money or I'll fucking cut your balls off, they say, and they've got an old blue Yankees hat with a hole in the top, and a faded blue jacket with a patch that says I LOVE NYC. They've also got a knife that says I LOVE TO CUT OFF YOUR BALLS. You're the same goddamn guy from last week, I say. The money, they say. No shit, I say, my balls, and I give them my wallet. Shit happens, they say, and all I'm thinking is Jesus Christ, I hate the subway.

When I get to the end of the red line, I step out of the car and trip, because there's a man lying there on the floor. He's got a full business suit and his briefcase is on the floor next to him. Watch the face, he says. You'll break my glasses. What are you, I say, goddamn crazy? I have a bad back, he says, my doctor says that I'm supposed to get people to step on it. It makes it feel better. But, I say, you're lying on your back. People will step on your stomach. Hey, he says, his face turning red, I didn't ask for your goddamn opinion. No shit, I say, and I head up the stairs. This whole goddamn city is nuts.

So I'm late by the time I get to the 7-Eleven. When I'm late, I go in the back door, but this is a small place, so by back door I mean the filthy little window in the men's room at the back of the store. I go around back, but there's an ass sticking out of the window. Mitch has lodged himself in there and there's no room. Jesus, Mitch, I say, is this where you've been? I'm stuck, he says, but really it's like his ass is talking. No shit, I say. I'm so hungry, he says. Jesus, Mitch, we all thought you quit, I say. No, he says, I've been here for a week. Humans can only survive without water for three days, I say. Oh, he says. For God's sake, I say, why didn't you just use the main entrance? I was late, he says. No shit, I say, so am I. Do you have any food? he says. No, I say, I just got mugged, almost lost my balls. No shit, he says. You're telling me, I say. Well you know what they say, he says. Don't you goddamn go there, I say, I'm going inside. Wait, he says, I'll die here if I don't get out soon. Shit happens, I say.

When I get inside the store, it's empty. There's not even a single goddamn Twinkie left. Someone has pillaged the place, alright. I run back outside to Mitch's ass. Mitch, I say, did you see anybody rob the store? Not that I can remember, he says. What about the boss, I say, did you see him? Well, he says, he hasn't come into the men's room, at least. Shit, I say. I think I'm dying, he says. Mitch, I say, now is not the time, and I run back inside. On my way in I trip and fall flat on my hands. I told you, says the man in the business suit, to watch the face. Now he's by the door to the 7-Eleven. What the hell, I say, are you following me? Please step on my back, he says, my doctor says I really need to have someone step on my back. I think you need to see a different doctor, I say, and then I kick him in the balls, and when he curls up into the fetal position, I roll him out of the store. Then I lock the door and sit down behind the counter.

I put my head in my hands. Jesus Christ, I say, what's wrong with this place? *Whosoever shall be ashamed of me and of my words*, says Jesus Christ, emerging from behind a rack normally stacked with crappy magazines, *of him shall the Son of man be ashamed*. Holy shit, I say. I figure it has to really be Him; He's a kind of scruffy-looking guy with a beard, but His head glows with the magnificent light of the heavens. *Whosoever therefore shall confess me before men*, he says, *him will I confess also before my Father which is in heaven*. Um, that's nice, I say. *Also*, He says, *I notice you're out of Twinkies*. No shit, I say, the whole place has been pillaged, there's nothing left. *Are you sure*, He says, *that there are no Twinkies? You don't keep them in storage, for example?* No, I say, all we have is what you see. *Shit*, He says, *I really like Twinkies*. Look, I say, I just told you, I don't have any goddamn Twinkies. He pauses for a minute. *Well*, He says, *could you at least spot me a twenty? I'm broke*. I just got mugged, I say, I don't have any money. *Well, you know what they say*, He says, and then I kick Him in the balls, and when He curls up into a fetal position, I roll Him out of the store.

I lock the door and sit behind the counter. Then I stand back up again, because there's a squished Twinkie on my pants. I peel it off and throw it in the trash can. I guess I could feel sorry for Jesus now, but what the hell, He's a man like the rest of us when you get down to it, and, you know, shit happens.

— David Weiss

Elementary Indiscretions

Carl's mother kept a collection of glass figurines high and dry over the kitchen sink. She was a broad-shouldered woman with a back like a breadboard and soft, meaty hands that could fold over Carl and redirect his breathing. Her name was Penfield and the figurines were vestiges of her youth and a thin-faced mother she no longer saw. Now the figurines overlooked a farmyard, dancing ladies lindy-hopping before a red barn, curtsying to the smell of crumbling hay.

When Carl got sent home from school she didn't know what to think. When one of her figurines went missing she marched big flat feet up the stairs and stood at the foot of Carl's bed. It was two in the afternoon and he was making rhythmic gulping noises with his breath. Her son the goldfish. She knew these weren't his sleeping sounds so she expelled the air from her lungs.

"Carl, I know you're awake." He kicked a leg but continued the breathing. "Carl, talk to me."

Muffling his voice with head to pillow, he shooed back up at her, "Go away." Penfield took a palm, wide as the side of a barn or the state of Nebraska, and got a hold of Carl's neck. He rose up sputtering for air, fish out of water and cat out of the bag.

"Where's my blue-glass lady with the ostrich plume fan?"

Across town and up from the river, Dan Carrol was getting off the school bus. Dan lived in a house hidden by trees, romped in a rural fortress yard. When he got off the bus, red hair radiant against its yellow siding, his dogs erupted in a trembling rush of sound. He craned his neck to see them beyond the trees. When the bus pulled away, Dan ran down, down the driveway, arms extended like an airplane in flight. Nobody saw him. He had sad, downturned eyes and lips that folded in. He looked strange and stoic and, running eagle-like, his face stood stamp-like, paradox to his flowing body.

At eleven that morning Dan had asked the girl at the desk across from him if she'd like to get hitched. "Will you marry me?" he asked, his eyes glazed with varnish or turpentine. She was nine, he was ten, and this was their third-grade classroom. A red digital clock over the door sang out 11:07. Behind Dan the heater whistled. He wasn't sure why he said what he said but now Tyler, to his left, was interested. The girl said, "I'm not old enough to get married." She wore her long hair with a green cloth headband. "Will you marry me?" Dan asked again. He smiled and his eyes stayed stock-still. The girl, who had thoughts of her own, said no. Dan turned on the face his mother told him looked like an angel and grinned at her all through the day.

"I don't know, Mom," Carl moaned. Carl's voice was the texture of a moan, or maybe a whirring carburetor. He kept his mouth wide open when he moaned.

"Don't give me that," said Penfield. If Carl moaned she didn't mince words. "And get out of bed. You're suspended, not on vacation." Carl swung out of bed and gave her his back. Moan moved to mumble.

"Not suspended," mumbled Carl, "sent home from school." Penfield breathed in a gallon or so of air and pushed out hot breath.

"You wrote dirty letters, Carl. Sex is not a laughing matter." She patted his knee with the resounding thumps of a leather hand. "Come downstairs and I'll make you grilled cheese and tuna." She left after giving him a meaningful look.

They had giggled when they found the letters, more perplexed than anything. The letters had been wedged in the white-wood cubbies like a forgotten lunch box. They were written to girls in the class, and they *were* the girls in the class. "Dear Christina," read Johanna, who always read such things aloud, green headband shining. The letters talked about butts and kissing, pulling pants down and shirts up. Some were carefully charted love maps. They were colorful but gave Johanna a bad shiver because the long looped writing belonged to Carl, who kept his mouth open and his eyebrows raised. She thought they were silly but a good find. The tall girl, Elise, tittered like an uncertain sapling. She did not want to think about such things, so she told her mother. The next day they sent Carl home early to sort things out.

Brooding now, Carl glowered over a quartered sandwich. Grilled cheese grease seeped into the creases on his hand. Penfield sat at the end of the table, eyes glued to her son. She didn't look at her hands while she ate. Behind her boy's bulbous head the figurines stood watch in the window. They tiptoed gracefully and made no noise, were soft like mice. "Sex is not to be taken lightly," boomed Penfield. Embarrassed, Carl turned his head. He wanted to play basketball, to dribble badly around the court and attempt a layup. He remembered writing letters with Dan on the kitchen floor and wondered why they'd only signed Carl's name.

Penfield had been outside chopping wood, staggering like a momma black bear in the autumn cold. With mixed intentions, Dan and Carl spilled markers on the braided rug. With a red crayola, Carl asked girls to meet him in the parking lot. It gave him a tingle to write it, but he couldn't imagine anything beyond the words. Dan drew black hearts and wrote, *Johanna plus Morgan equals sex*. He told Carl some things to write. Standing by the window over the kitchen sink, Dan saw Penfield by the barn, arms raised over a sturdy neck as she split logs with an ax. He thought of his mother, thin back straight as she watched the evening news. He'd seen her split her face with a smile when his father brought home a new VCR. Sun streamed through the glass interior of a dancing figurine. The dancer's fan spewed out light, and if Dan moved his head, she covered Penfield completely. He stood this way, mouth agape, for quite some time.

Outside by the picnic table Johanna told her friend Susie the meaning of oral sex. Susie swapped it for *retard*. Johanna watched movies where teenagers screwed like bunnies, but they said *special* in her house. "Slut," said Peter Chidsey out on the swings. The set was blue and the swings yellow. "Pussy," said Jenn Basil, giggling by the apple tree. "Will you marry me?" said Dan Carrol.

"Take her to a scary movie and she'll jump in your lap."

"Ask her to have sex with you."

"My little honey bear."

"A slut," said Peter, "is a lady who has sex with anyone without making them pay." He spun around the chains on the swing.

"Pussy," said Jenn Basil, "is a girl's *you know*. Her *thing*." She motioned down to illustrate the point.

"Will you marry me?" said Dan Carrol.

Dan was an orange face and sad eyes. On the last day of school he pushed her a box. It felt heavy and smelled of ostrich plumes.

Looking over the farm, Penfield felt the rumbling of a roar. Her shoulders tumbled down, boulders from mountaintops. She was losing the battle faster than she would have supposed.

— Johanna Povirk-Znoy

Our Thursday

For we brought nothing into this world,
and it is certain we can carry nothing out.
                              I Timothy 6:7

The world is so quiet.
The story of our lives is a life, a death.

A poem so normal it fades.
She passed away.

Why do they say that,
implying the from and to?

An Australian phone call,
a rip in my side,

I heard a bomb ticking and I ran up the stairs
and covered my ears.

All these years I'd believed my mother
would cry, these muddy, oily puddles just

jutting, dividing mascara. It would be the
first time. There were no tears.

Oh, these years, a strangled foresight,
anticipation choked like a stone in there.

My sister and I, alone.
This world is so quiet. Ungenerous.

All I can give you
is an itch in my nose,

six years of not seeing you, what
more can I do?

"Just listen. It's peace lilies for funerals."
Behind-the-scenes bereavement,

diaspora of the family. "Do this for your
mother," said my mother to her sister.

The old woman sat in the chair
in the quiet house in her body

the heart stopped and she died.
Wiry hair short inches from the scalp,

thin silk shirts, my limbs remember
the age of that nearness.

And so your last years were my
first years and I wanted to know

was it worth it.
In my infant drag queen days,

it was the heat that made me do it,
you wheeled this star in the throne of his stroller.

God, she watches my every move so I'll only make
the best mistakes

but our sin has always been
the willingness to forget.

The Bible says she went to hell because
she prayed to gods with oranges.

These clairvoyant voyeur angels
when I finally start having sex.

I stare at my shoes in your honor,
I wear my mourning colors.

For you I listened to all the sad records
so my eyes would be wet sometimes for you.

But no one comes to rescue.
The world is still ungenerous.

Girls cluster with airy voices
and gift wrap words for

the girl behind me, her boyfriend, he
street raced and lies on the gurney.

Don't be empty with no
pity, lonely without a shoulder.

At whom does this poem genuflect —
your life? my strength?

Clandestine "Has mom cried yet?"
The "From where?" and the "Where to?"

Everything I will see right through.
I'll see through the memory on my way back to you for the

someday that I might know you because it never is
too late.

— Andrew Chan

Nyiav to My Mother

I nod curtly as he leaves the room, giving me and my mother some privacy. I look around the doctor's office. I feel uncomfortable in the warm room. How do you tell your mother she is dying and you, her oldest son, can do nothing to save her? Sons rarely sit this close to their mothers, especially at my age. And I realize how old my mother has gotten. Her hair is grayer and her eyes wiser, darker. She clasps her hands together in a tight ball on her lap. My poor mother, so old in her ways. The cancer is in her body, spreading fast, Dr. Reynolds said. And my mother sat there, nodding as if she understood the American telling her she was going to die. But she doesn't get it, not like I do.

I had told her that we should make an appointment at the clinic months ago when I first noticed her illness but she was so against the idea she called my younger brother and he talked me out of it. Both of them argued that the doctors would blow her illness out of proportion, claim she had some deadly disease and would die a horrible death. I said they wouldn't.

To heal the sickness, my mother had my brother sacrifice a chicken and tie white strings around her hand, representing the spirits that would carry away the evil surrounding her. When it seemed that the strings had let her down, she attended a Catholic church with me. She even sang the songs with me. And I finally took her to visit a doctor.

"*Niam*," I whisper, our word for *mother*.

She turns to me slowly and shakes her head at me. She makes me a boy again when she stares at me so intently with her brown eyes. She can always do that. There are times when I want her to

209

hold me like she did in the past, when things were at peace and the war had not yet begun and had not reached our village, when my father was alive and hunting and I, a boy, did the playing and we all did the laughing. Twenty years ago seems too far, unreachable, as I sit staring at her pale face.

"I told you," she says in Hmong. She had understood the doctor. "You never listen to your brother and me."

The doctor comes in shortly after and asks if he can do anything. He tells me they'll start treatment as soon as possible. They want my mother to stay overnight. I look over to her and I wonder if the doctor wondered why I hadn't yet reached out to hold her hand. I simply shake my head. My mother is going to go home.

In the car, she is quiet. I am not expecting such a mood from her because she is an outspoken person. But as I think about it, it seems perfectly fine. The silence continues to ascend much like the bitter cold blowing through the broken heater.

The car dies before I can properly park it. I was never really good at driving stick shift. I close my eyes and shake my throbbing head. My mother closes the car door lightly and makes her way to the house. Usually, she'd slam the door in haste, grumble about the chill, and go in search of the comfort of her slippers. I don't hear the grumble and I don't see the quickness in her step. She takes off her shoes and carries them in one lonely hand into the house. I already miss her.

My wife is lying in our bed, her arms encircling our baby boy. It isn't even dark yet, and I am so tired. My older children are out somewhere in this state of California, and I am not even mad. I remember walking into the kitchen after the appointment with the doctor and telling my wife about my mother's condition. Her eyes watered so quickly I left the kitchen. I called my younger brother and the next day he showed up at my door, suitcase in hand. My mother wasn't surprised when he came because she knew my brother had a gentle heart. I knew he could bring her the spirits and the medicine I left a long time ago. I was simply the older brother, eldest son born to take care of the family. That was my role.

I had thought about my mother's request during dinner. I remember staring at the steam from the rice bowl, making her words into a clear picture. I could see what she was saying and what she had dreamed for so long, and I knew that I could give my mother this gift as she had given me so many. If she wanted to die in Laos, surrounded by the mountains of her homeland, I would give her that.

Now I slip into bed and reach for the lamp beside my wife's sleeping head. My son's hair is wet from my wife's tears, and I frown.

The passports come a little over two weeks later. My mother's, my brother's, and mine are all together when they arrive. When I hold mine to the light, I can see the eagle and the reflecting gold, blue, and green colors across my picture. I remember how nervous I was, standing behind the white line. I remember the sweat sliding over my fingertips.

"On the count of three, sir," the red-haired boy said. He held up his hand as if he were a conductor in a black tuxedo guiding a great choir. "One. Two. Three."

I wasn't as ready as I wanted to be, but the flash broke my concentration and a smile appeared on my lips.

It is about three days before the big drive from Fresno to LA. It will take a little over five hours, depending on traffic, to get to the airport. I am planning our route right now. We will travel from LA to Hong Kong, Hong Kong to Bangkok, and Bangkok to Vientiane. From the capital of Laos, we'll take a taxi and, finally, walk to our village.

The doctor refused when I told him about this trip, but I begged and prayed he'd change his mind. Dr. Reynolds has always been a kind man to our community and he understands the importance of this. I write his name down on the sheet of paper beside my world map. I must make sure to thank him.

Many of my cousins are over at my house. They're giving us clothes and money to give to their fallen relatives in Laos. I can only accept these things, stuff them alongside everyone else's and hope I don't forget.

My mother isn't getting any better. She complains about her bones and her eyes. She tells me she is going blind. I sigh. I am planning the whole trip; everything will be fine. And when we arrive in Laos, everything will be even better. I am excited about this trip, not because I am able to go back to my homeland but because my brother is not excited. He has never seen Laos before, except for pictures and videos. I will get to show him my knowledge of the Hmong world. I am not too American to forget the ways of my people. I am not too old to forget.

*   *   *

We are stuck in traffic. This is California traffic and I am driving a stick shift. My mother is telling me she is sick and my brother is telling me how to drive. I nod to the both of them and smile at the other drivers pulling up beside me and those who drive past me. I point at a few signs to show my mother how close the airport is. She nods at me and pulls her coat collar closer around her neck.

"Are you cold?" I ask.

She shakes her head and points toward the approaching building. The huge white arcs crossing at the center, the moving buses, and the massive crowds are so captivating I don't want to look at the road. I want to park somewhere, run inside, and fly to Laos, directly to Laos. The rush of my blood is tremendous, and I smile at my brother. He smiles back. In the backseat, my mother coughs and marvels at the flying plane above my stick shift car.

"Are you okay?" I ask in Hmong. "Why don't you sit down."

My mother's breathing quickens and her eyes, she says, are getting darker. The drive and the walk from the front door, through the metal detectors, and to our terminal has worn her out. It takes us a long time to find Terminal 2. People rush by the three of us as we stare out the huge glass windows. A plane sounds from outside, then another one. When we arrive, Terminal 2 is empty of people and suitcases.

"*Niam*, you rest here," my brother says, pointing to a chair. He looks at me. "I'm going to the bathroom. *Hu dab laug*. Call Uncle."

I look around the airport and sigh. I remember when I arrived in America. I was five and my brother wasn't born yet. My father was dead and my mother had sworn to him that she'd never marry again. We had come with my mother's brother's family, and so my mother and I were safe. There had been so many people in the airport that day and everyone and everything was stacked and bundled together. It wasn't cozy. I had never heard so many languages before, all languages I did not speak. When my uncle found me, I was crying. He promised me he'd take care of me just as he had promised his widowed sister a better life in America. I often wondered if there was more to it than simply her brother's promise. Perhaps under the sun in Laos I resembled my father too much and his country could offer me no more peace. I don't remember my father dying.

My mother's head falls on my shoulder. Doesn't she know people are looking? They pass by, aware we are mother and son, but do not know of our journey together. They wouldn't understand her head on my shoulder. I gently shake her.

"*Niam*," I whisper. I shake her again. "*Sawv nas.* Wake up."

I notice her slouching and I know that she never slouches; it is a terrible thing for women to do. But the chair she is sitting in has already engulfed her body, and her head hangs low in the air. I look around. My brother has to come back from the bathroom soon, and I need to make a phone call to my wife, to hear her voice.

I remember my first day in church, singing the songs so loud. After the boys carried the candles outside and the priest followed with the cross, I knelt in a pew and bowed my head. Tears didn't fall from my eyes but I did see water, water so clear I saw my father. We were laughing in our bamboo home, the dirt swept neatly beneath our stools. I knew my father was as pleased with me in the church as he would have been if I had stayed in Laos. He wanted me to sing.

I hold my mother's head near my heart. I hope she can hear it beating. She has given me her mountains and she has given me my home. I lower my lips to her ear and mumble words only she can hear, words only her spirits can understand. I gently hum my *nyiav*, my hymn of her life, to her.

— Kao Nou Thao

After the Snowstorm

Tonight, I collect the things I miss
in small, measured bundles. What I know
hangs from my eyelids in long lists.

Workmen in parkas retrieve downed power lines. I insist
on waiting for you on the porch as the snow
collects. I think about the things I miss:

leaning backwards in your arms. Small kisses
in heavy traffic, or the curved bow
of your lips against my eyelids at night. Those long lists

that I shovel together. They pile in drifts:
making love on picnic tables, short notes you wrote
in a hurried hand. A small collection. How could I miss

the signs of waning love over so short a time? This
may be the last time I wait for you. I am growing
cold; I shut my eyes, breathe on my hands. Do you miss

my warmth beside you at night or the lists
we made of places to travel? Here: throw
them with mine. They collect like the snow
on my eyelashes: the things we miss in ordered rows.

— Brittany Cavallaro

Sugar

I.

There were icicles hanging from the freezer. It was continuously breaking and fixing itself again, as the ice melted and refroze. She stood on her tiptoes as she opened the fridge door, the light blinking three times before turning on for good, sending veins of fluorescent glow across the thin skin of her cheeks. She gazed, awestruck by the glistening icicles hanging from the shiny white plastic ice machine; they looked as sweet as the ice pops she stole from her grandmother's back freezer, though these icicles seemed even more brilliant, glittering magically from the top shelf, dangling alluringly above the ice tray. In one sudden motion she reached out toward it, her tongue darting from between her lips to taste the frozen metallic water splices. They shivered her taste buds, making her want to pull back in shock. She reared her head, but the movement sent a wave of throbbing from her tongue as it stuck tightly to the lustrous metallic plastic. That was when she remembered her mother's warning.

"Don't try to lick the ice, dear. You'll get stuck to it."

"OK, Mama," she had sighed at yet another constraint. The recollection made her try again fretfully to remove her head from where it stuck to the freezer, anticipating her mother's plodding heels rounding the kitchen doorway at any moment. Her ears were beginning to prickle; the ice machine had switched off again, and its silence filled her with apprehension. Her eyes were watering, flitting hot drips of saltiness down her cheeks that became frosty as they reached her chinbone. The chapped insides of her nose ached slightly as she breathed in the icicle grit. A piece of the icicle, far below her, dropped in one small bead. She saw the droplet distinctly, even with her eyes crossed. The sounds of footsteps seemed to be growing louder as they collided with the wooden floorboards. And then another drip came. Her eyes ached. She let her gaze slip ahead and stared at the glittering plastic. The sticky air stretched along her calves as they hung out the open door, and she could feel her toes becoming white from the pressure of her body weight. The drips were coming faster now, proliferating. Suddenly, the ice became milky in her mouth and she felt her tongue slide off, pulling her body down again. She immediately craned to see the sugary white glisteners again and let the gulp out from her numbed face as her mother rounded the corner.

II.

A peach's sugar develops softly, diffusing into the softening skin. It is the inverse of a baby's growth, reverting to tenderness from the calloused shell that began it. The sharp body becomes muddy and succulent, imparting a juicy bouquet. To her it smelled strangely similar to, but richer and realer than, the "fresh peach" deodorant she had started to apply each morning. She inhaled to taste the brown, mellifluous sugar, filling her nose with the aroma of a sticky fructose. She sat perched on the kitchen counter, the plywood straining under her growing thighs. Her heels knocked against the wooden cabinets beneath her, sending vibrations through her thudding toes. She lifted the mushy peach to her hand, its honey-suckled distillation nearly collapsing onto her baggy T-shirt as she held it between thumb and nail. She drank in the juice from beneath its fragile skin, the pores along the peach down widening as she sucked in the beads. The countertop groaned slightly as she swallowed, as if longing to partake of the syrupy nectar. She bit into the mud of its core, letting its sugar warm her teeth with its cakey softness. She could smell its completion before it came, her teeth hitting the pit's ridges, disappointed, although she knew it was inevitable. Quietly, her legs slid off the countertop, muggy toes sticking as they landed on the humid linoleum floor tiles. She left drops from the ambrosia behind her on the plywood for the counter to absorb as she slipped over to the faucet.

III.

Her grandmother craved root beer in her last days. She asked for tall glasses of it, filled with ice, the smell of sassafras root bubbling over the edges of the cup. No one knew why she craved it so much. Maybe she had always craved it, or maybe she had developed a taste for it, as she had developed a taste for the chemo as it entered her through a built-in tap over her breastbone. No matter what, they wanted her to have root beer. They bought packs of it at the Bi-Lo, hoping to nurse her on it until she was able to stand on her own again, to rise from her bed without someone else's legs boosting her up, to walk without stumbling. Of course, they knew root beer wouldn't make her well again, but they gave it to her anyway, nursing her gently, preparing her taste buds for the sweetness of the next world.

— Emrys Jaskwhich

Asterisk

A star, fallen from above.

Not quite good enough to perch atop this world's purple-black night sky.

Never again will it shine its light down from the darkened heavens

Giving an unearthly glow to the slush in the gutters

On a night when steam rises from the manhole covers in the streets

When the only audible sound is a single far-off car driving toward somewhere else

And one by one, the lofty skyscraper deities close their many illuminated
eyes.

It has been banned from the mellow life of a star.

No more can it help guide a cold, tired traveler.

It has been assigned to the worldly task of punctuation.

Its sole job to remind us that there is a catch.

Something else we must consider.

One last fact.

Yet it still sits just a little bit higher than the other letters,

Waiting for the day when the message will be delivered

That it can return to its life as a star

And calmly sit on top of it all

And watch the world go to sleep.

— Tim Horgan-Kobelski

THE SCHOLASTIC
ART & WRITING AWARDS

program of the Alliance for Young Artists & Writers, Inc.

If you're a student in grades 7-12 in the United States or Canada, you could win one of 50,000 local and 1,100 national awards in 25 categories, including 11 cash grants of $10,000 each, and more than $1.55 million in scholarships.

The Alliance for Young Artists & Writers invites young writers, artists, designers, photographers, animators and moviemakers to enter the longest-running annual competition of its kind in North America.

Get full details at **www.artandwriting.org**

PUSH

YOU ARE HERE.

www.thisispush.com

Meet the authors.
        Read the books.
ell us what you want to see.
        Submit your own words.
Read the words of others.

this is PUSH.

PUSH YOU ARE HERE.

IN STORES NOW

****

BE A PUSH AUTHOR.
WRITE NOW.

Enter the PUSH Novel Contest for a chance to get your novel published. You don't have to have written the whole thing — just sample chapters and an outline. For full details, check out the contest area on *www.thisispush.com*

****